Thomas James Mumford

Life and letters of Thomas J. Mumford

With special memorial tributes

Thomas James Mumford

Life and letters of Thomas J. Mumford
With special memorial tributes

ISBN/EAN: 9783337134648

Printed in Europe, USA, Canada, Australia, Japan

Cover: Foto ©Raphael Reischuk / pixelio.de

More available books at **www.hansebooks.com**

LIFE AND LETTERS

OF

THOMAS J. MUMFORD,

WITH

MEMORIAL TRIBUTES.

BOSTON:

GEORGE H. ELLIS, 101 MILK STREET.

1879.

Stereotyped and Printed by

GEO. H. ELLIS,

101 Milk Street, Boston.

CONTENTS.

INTRODUCTION.

To those who knew and loved Thomas J. Mumford, this little book will need no justification. They will welcome it, not simply as a tribute to his memory, but as a fresh and genial manifestation of his spirit. There is not one who knew him well who may not find here an opportunity to know him better. In the letters which furnish nearly one-half of the contents of this book, they will recognize in the touch and charm of his gifted pen, new exhibitions of his playful wit, his earnestness of character, his strength of conviction, his heroic devotion to the truth, his unwavering conscientiousness, and that sweetness of heart which gave a rich aroma to his whole life. And many of those who knew him not according to the flesh may delight to find in the revelations of his higher life that deeper touch of moral nature which makes the whole world kin. They will recognize a friend whom they would like to have known, as the visitor in a picture gallery is now and then charmed and taken into the friendship of some one revealing face, or as Paul loved the Jesus whom he had never seen.

Those who were fortunate enough to have Mr. Mumford as a pastor found ready access to the inner temple. The rare gifts of his nature had, in this relationship, free scope for personal expression. In the hearts of those whom he had thus helped and served, there are tender memories which this book could hardly supplement. But the far wider circle of those who knew him only as an editor had not an equal advantage. They could feel the pressure of mind and heart in every number of his bright and attractive paper; for Mr. Mumford in his sphere as editor had an unusual power of making himself felt without allowing himself to be seen. Yet there were few who, appreciating his editorial work, did not suspect that the man was more than the editor, and who did not really lose in their distance from him even more than they suspected.

It is no disparagement to Mr. Mumford's success that he was known far more widely by his work than he was by his name. Few editors were so quotable as he. Many of his best paragraphs were reset and reprinted in other journals, which introduced him frequently to a large circle of readers who never knew the author, but who certainly felt his influence. Just how widely he was known and appreciated as an editor did not appear until his life was closed. Then the flood of notices from the religious press, representing all denominations and all sections of our country, revealed the depth and extent and nature of the impression which his editorial work had made. The unanimity of this impression, and the cordiality with which it was acknowledged, furnish a striking proof of the genuineness of the man and the effectiveness of his work. At the close of this volume, the reader will find some of the cut flowers which his editorial brethren far and near scattered so profusely over his tomb.

Mr. Mumford's name and fame might safely rest in the work which he did and the recognition it received; but we feel sure that there are many beyond the range of his intimate personal friends who will be glad to learn something more of the growth and development through which it was achieved.

"Every man his own Boswell," is the motto of the "Autocrat of the Breakfast Table." We doubt, however, if Mr. Mumford could ever have been induced to write an autobiography. But in the letters which are presented in this volume, he has unconsciously furnished us the best kind of auto-biography. They were not written for the public eye. The writer had no suspicion that they were even to be preserved. They were addressed to inti-mate friends,— the majority to his spiritual father and guide, the Rev. Samuel J. May,— at periods of life ranging from youth to manhood. They were the fresh, spontaneous utterances of an active intellect and an affectionate heart. Arranged in chronological order, they furnish an almost con-nected account of his life from childhood until within a week of his death. They reveal the struggling and aspiring youth, the eager and indus-trious student, the kind husband and father, the earnest preacher, the tender pastor, and the brilliant journalist.

It has been the aim, in arranging these letters, to let them speak for themselves. All editorial matter, except that which was necessary to link them together, has been excluded. No attempt has been made to form a complete collection of Mr. Mumford's letters. If this had been the object, the present collection might well be deemed incomplete. He was a prompt and faithful correspondent, and many of his friends who read this book can claim bundles of letters which they will regard as of equal value with any it contains. The preponderance which is given to the letters addressed to the Rev. Samuel J. May will need no explanation wherever the beautiful relationship which subsisted between them is known. The story of that friendship he told briefly as he stood near Mr. May's grave : —

"Born in Beaufort District, South Carolina, where four-fifths of the inhabitants were slaves, the son of a slave-holder, until I was twenty years old I believed in slavery as a divine institution, and carried a Bible in my pocket to defend it against all comers. When the faithful hands of noble Quaker women removed the sacred veil which had concealed the monstrous features of the system, and I saw clearly at last that it was not of celestial but infernal origin, I soon lost all faith in my religious teachers, who seemed to declare that man was made for the Church and not the Church for man. I was almost drowning in a sea of scepticism, when Samuel J. May came to the town in Western New York where I lived.

"As soon as I saw his radiant face and heard his sweet yet earnest voice, I felt drawn to him by a mighty magnetism. It became my first desire to share in the blessed work that he was doing, to follow him, although with feeble steps and a great way off, in going about doing good. Since that day, all of my life that I can look back upon without regret and shame I owe to the inspiration of his example and the power of his encouragement. No other friend has exerted such an uplifting influence upon my spirit. Therefore I could not resist the strong attraction which has drawn me here to-day."

It was this strong and abiding attraction in the character of the distinguished reformer which impelled Mr. Mumford, at the urgent request also of Mr. May's friends and executors, to write the life of his spiritual counsellor and benefactor. The letters in this volume may properly be considered as a sequel to that work. They throw light, not merely upon the character of him who wrote them, but also upon the character of the noble man who inspired them. They show in what way that friendship was formed, and into what a tender union it ripened. We cannot but feel that all who rejoice in a frank, manly, earnest, and devout nature will find assistance in reading these warm and guileless exhalations of a pure and consecrated heart. They furnish a high yet normal key to which every young and aspiring life should be tuned.

The second part of the book is made up of the personal and biographical tributes which were published in a few numbers of *The Christian Register* immediately after Mr. Mumford's death, together with the friendly notices from the press which that event called forth. Interesting details and portraiture of life not revealed in his letters may be found in a biographical sketch by the Rev. Rush R. Shippen and in the sermon of Mr. Chadwick. These papers have been revised to adapt them to the more permanent record of this book, while the addresses made at the funeral have been preserved in the same free and spontaneous form in which they were caught by the stenographer's pen.

There is still another tribute tenderly recorded in this book to which it is most pleasing to revert. It is that which is silently expressed in the love and respect borne for Mr. Mumford by the publisher, his intimate friend and associate, and also by all those who have assisted in its mechanical preparation. This part of the work has been committed to no strange hands. It has been set up and printed by those who knew him well, who had so often followed his copy, and who were glad to pay him a printer's tribute of respect by the faithful use of the very same types whose imprint he so constantly read. No more cordial relation ever subsisted between editor and publisher, or between editor and printers and proof-readers, than subsisted between Mr. Mumford and his co-workers on the paper. *The Christian Register* was one of the first papers in Boston upon which women compositors were regularly employed. Mr. Mumford was a warm champion of this innovation, and was fond of pointing to its success. He was proud of the "girls," as he called them, and the acknowledged excellence of the typographical work of the *Register* shows that his pride was well founded. It is not surprising, then, that those whose interests he had so much at heart should delight to illustrate in his honor the fidelity and graces of that art through whose aid he achieved his highest success.

In the harmonious union in this threnody of the voice of him, who being dead yet speaketh, with the antiphonal song of those friends, — teachers, parishioners, brother-ministers, fellow-editors, and co-workers — who have gathered around his grave, there is blended in low undertone the minor strain of her who above all others has most right to mourn. Writing most of the editorial connectives, furnishing the facts for others, suggesting and selecting the letters which so well reveal his spirit, she has brought, like one of old, her sweet spices and ointment to tenderly embalm the memory of him whose spirit can no more be contained in the grave than could the spirit of him from whose tomb the angel rolled away the stone.

S. J. BARROWS.

LIFE AND LETTERS.

LIFE AND LETTERS OF THOMAS J. MUMFORD.

I.

REVIEW OF EARLY LIFE.

First Letter to Samuel J. May. — Story of his Youth. — Aspires to the Ministry. — Zeal for Reform.

WATERLOO, N.Y., Jan. 8, 1849.

REV. S. J. MAY:

Dear Sir,— Permit a stranger to ask a favor of you. I wish to know what peculiar qualifications are necessary to fit a candidate for the ministry of the Unitarian Church, the nature and extent of the preparation, the places where the studies may be pursued, and the plan of the Cambridge Divinity School. If you will send me an answer to these inquiries, I will thank you most heartily. Trusting that you will pardon the liberty I have taken, I am,

With great respect, your humble serv't,

THOMAS J. MUMFORD.

P.S.— If you are willing to listen, I will be glad to inform you of my reasons for asking the questions above, and to avail myself of your instruction and advice.

WATERLOO, N.Y., Jan. 21, 1849.

Dear Sir,— Your kind letter of the 11th inst. was duly received. The extracts from the "Register"

contained the information that I desired, and I thank you for your prompt compliance with my request.

Agreeably to your suggestions, I shall now write an explanation of my object in consulting you; and that it may be intelligible, I will preface it with a brief narrative of the most important events of my past life.

I am now twenty-two years of age. I am a native of South Carolina, but have resided in this place for eleven years. I have received an ordinary academical education. I left school in 1844, and entered upon the study of the law. After I had almost completed my preparatory studies, I abandoned the idea of becoming a lawyer. My reasons for so doing were twofold : I had become slightly deaf, and thus unfitted for successful practice at the bar, and I was sorely disappointed in the nature of legal practice. I could not reconcile myself to that indiscriminate advocacy of the right and the wrong which seems to be required by the present state of the profession. Last spring I became one of the editors and publishers of the *Seneca County Courier*, the old Whig organ of this county. Soon after I entered upon my editorial career, I was compelled to choose between interest and duty. Gen. Taylor was nominated, and I promptly refused to support him. About the first of September, I was compelled to sell my paper to the more orthodox Whigs. This act was performed with reluctance; but I could not afford to make any more pecuniary sacrifices, even for the cause of Freedom. I now intend, for several years at least, to pursue the editorial calling; but I am not sure that duty does not call me to another station.

For many years, I have been impressed with a belief that I ought to devote myself to the work of elevating the popular standard of morality, and disseminating correct ideas of the nature and laws of God. My parents were Episcopalians (my father, who died three years since, being a warden in the church, superintendent of the Sunday-school, etc.); and almost all my friends and relations are members of the various "orthodox" societies. Ever since I became conscious of responsibility, I have endeavored to observe all the rules of morality, and to cherish a sense of reverence and love for the Supreme Being; and when at the academy I attracted some notice as a speaker on several public occasions, my parents and others, observing my deportment, thought me calculated for the work of the Christian ministry. Accordingly, I was frequently urged by my much-beloved friend, the Rev. Mr. Wheeler, to prepare for the pulpit. Many inducements were held out to me, and I should probably have followed the bent of their inclination, and to some extent my own, had I been satisfied with the doctrines of the Church. But I was not satisfied, and I could not play the hypocrite.

I have read and thought much on the subject of Christian doctrine for several years past, and the effect of my investigation and reflection is a warm attachment to the principles of the Unitarian Christians, as set forth in the writings of Dr. Channing.

I have been so unfortunate as to differ with some

of my most beloved relatives and many of my kindest friends upon several vital questions. They are slaveholders; I am an ardent hater of the accursed system of human bondage. They are Whigs, ever loyal to their party. In my opinion, the Whig party has belied its noble anti-slavery professions, and in the late contest I found myself compelled to act against it, or stifle the voice of conscience. And, lastly, they are "orthodox," and I am Unitarian.

Now, although I do not hesitate to think and do what I believe to be right on account of these differences, I find that their dislike of my views is, in some particulars, a serious hindrance to my progress. They think I have rashly thrown away a fine chance to obtain political honor and offices; and should I immediately begin to study for the Unitarian ministry, I fear that I should hazard even their friendship. They would regard me as one seeking to become an instrument of evil and heresy, and would probably be as unwilling to grant as I should be indisposed to ask any "aid and comfort," pecuniary or spiritual. I can, however, obtain enough money to defray my expenses at Meadville, if the published statement be true.

I have determined to devote myself to the work of religious, moral, and political reformation; and I am only at a loss to decide in which station I can be most useful,— the newspaper office or the pulpit. If my decision be in favor of the latter, I shall endeavor to earn my living and a part of the means of prosecuting my studies, even though my entrance upon my future duties should be considerably postponed. But I am not entirely satisfied that it will not be better for me to remain an editor.

If the learning required at the Cambridge Divinity School be a "condition precedent" to the ministry, I hardly know how I can now master it. I have already spent three years in studying for one profession. I have always been a diligent and careful reader, and I think I may justly claim to an extensive acquaintance with English literature, and some familiarity with political history and the great movements of the present day. While at school I was perhaps too much interested in the events of the present, and too much inclined to "let the dead past bury its dead"; for I valued the Latin and Greek only as helps to a better knowledge of the English. I would like the study of the German, I think, and would apply myself to the task of learning so much of the dead languages as may be absolutely necessary to a proper preparation for the ministry.

Will you oblige me by writing your opinion upon this matter of "classical learning" in connection with the studies for the ministry?

I am, with great respect, your friend,

THOMAS J. MUMFORD.

P.S.— I acknowledge that the chief reason of my wish to stand in the pulpit arises from a painful conviction that the present popular standard of morality is lamentably low. If I become a minister, I shall devote much of my attention to the popular sins of the day, repudiating all such atheistical maxims as "my country (or my party), right or wrong," and striving to be *for* the right, whoever may oppose it ; *against* the wrong, whoever may uphold it. I think the pulpits of our country are wanting in ministers bold enough to do this, and hope that I am among the number who are ready to reinforce the gallant band who now defend Freedom and Truth against such fearful odds.

I know the dangers and difficulties of such a course, but trust that an ardent love of righteousness, and rigid economy will, with the Divine aid, enable me to wage a manly warfare against the giant evils of our time and nation.

Rev. S. J. May.

II.

CHOICE OF THE MINISTRY.

The Decision Made. — Spirit of Sacrifice. — Notes of his Reading. — Opposition from Friends.

Feb. 1, 1849.

Dear Sir,— After the gravest deliberation of which my mind is capable, I am well convinced that my place is in the pulpit, and that I ought to enter upon the work of preparation immediately. Your kind interest in my welfare has excited my liveliest gratitude, and an early reply to the inquiry I am about to make will be most pleasing and serviceable to me.

Upon referring to the leaves of the "Register," for which I am indebted to you, I perceive that a term of the Meadville School will commence in about a fortnight from this time. I am anxious to enter upon the duties of the ministry as soon as I may be fitted therefor, and no sooner; and I think that by commencing immediately, the end I have in view will be more speedily attained. What shall I do,— go to Meadville the middle of this month, or study at home until September? If it will hasten my preparation, I prefer the former course; and my business here requires that I shall have at least a fortnight's notice of the fact. I have broached my purposes to my family and to some of my friends. The former assent, only regretting that I am not to be the advocate of their faith. Some of the latter with whom I have conversed about the expense of time and money which will be incurred, hint that most clergymen are starved into silence concerning popular sins, etc.; but I tell them I will be content with a moderate share of this world's goods, if I can only live a true life, serving God and doing good to my fellow-men. Is it unreasonable to suppose that an earnest, industrious, and competent minister can somewhere find hearers and the means of living?

March 8, 1849.

My dear Friend,— Agreeably to the promise made at the close of the pleasant visit which I enjoyed at your house a few weeks since, I will now write an account of my progress and prospects.

My strong dislike of pecuniary dependence has led me to accept several offers of brief but lucrative employment, and therefore I have not, according to my purpose at the time of our last conversation, devoted all of my time to study.

Out of the course which you have so kindly suggested, I have read the first volume of Macaulay's History, Channing's essay on "The Duty of the Free States," his letter on "Creeds," and several of his discourses. Among the last, I have experienced most exquisite pleasure in reading those entitled "Christianity a Rational Religion," "The Church," and "Spiritual Freedom." These breathe the spirit which I trust animates me, and their trains of thought have often passed through my own mind. I am, of course, in many respects at a vast distance from Dr. Channing; but I am near enough to know and feel and rejoice that there is between us a pure and joyous spiritual communion. In the writings of no other man do I meet with thoughts that find so perfect an echo in my highest convictions of right, and so cordial a response in my noblest sense of duty. I feel that I cannot be too grateful to Heaven for having sent such a hero soul before me, and I know of no better way of evincing my gratitude than by emulating to the uttermost verge of my ability his bright and lofty example.

I have also read Parker's sermon on "The Idea of a Christian Church," with which I was much pleased. The fresh, vigorous, and free style with which his keen perceptions of the beautiful, the true, and the absurd compel him to clothe his thoughts, gives a charm to his writings which will always secure them many delighted readers; but I prefer the closer reasoning and the more tranquil (and yet not less strong and triumphant) faith which distinguish the works of Channing.

I have also read Mr. Furness' sermon on "The Nature and Uses of Public Worship," delivered in New York and published in the *Tribune* about a fortnight ago. His thoughts are mine, and I think you will not object to any of them. In any event, I shall be glad to learn your opinion.

Sunday mornings I devote to the reading of the Scriptures. In the afternoons, I attend Episcopal service with the other members of my family. A few Sundays since, my good friend Mr. M. preached an able and most pointed sermon against Unitarianism. He relied mainly on the text which inquires how Christ could be both David's Lord and Son. Many of my friends call the discourse triumphant; but they have only heard the advocate of one side of the question.

As I expected, I am somewhat annoyed by the horror expressed, with uplifted hands and mournful voice, by some of my friends when they speak of the awful peril to which I have exposed my soul. Their frequent allusions to my father's orthodoxy in contrast with my heterodoxy, although doubtless well meant, are not always either delicate or agreeable. But what are these petty trials compared with the self-contempt which attends the profession of a faith which the reason rejects, and to which the heart will not respond? No person who knows what Unitarianism is has yet attacked me, and I am glad of it. I want my time for undisturbed study and reflection upon truths which even bigots believe and neglect. Although prone to well-conducted debate, I do not desire to erect the structure of my theological education, after the manner of certain builders of old, with a trowel in one hand and a sword in the other, and I trust I shall be spared the disagreeable necessity. At the same time, however, I am not ashamed of my faith, and shall not shrink from its vindication on all proper occasions.

III.

PREPARING FOR MEADVILLE.

Interest in his Studies. — Paley Arraigned. — Anti-Slavery Sympathies. — Ideal of the Ministry. — Theological Discussions.

March 22, 1849.

Dear Friend,— During the last fortnight, I have studied constantly and satisfactorily. I have read Paley's "Natural Theology" with the most careful attention, and think I have obtained a pretty thorough knowledge of the work. The edition which I read contains notes by Sir Charles Bell, Lord Brougham, and Dr. — now Bishop — Potter. In connection with Paley's chapters on the subject, I read many pages in several works on physiology. In the "Theology" I have found much to admire, and some things to which I cannot now assent. Those passages which seem to imply a belief that the slaughter of human beings on the field of battle is one of God's provisions for counteracting the superfecundity of our species shocked me most. I have always disliked the school of writers who advocate the theory of population broached, I believe, by Malthus, and in part indorsed by Dr. Chalmers.

I am surprised that the clear-sighted Paley countenanced the horrible idea that war is one of the heaven-appointed means of ridding countries of their surplus inhabitants. It seems to me that a Christian statesman would find in emigration and the breaking up of immense landed estates a much more effective and far less objectionable cure for the evil.

Do you not think the "Theology" incomplete? A system of "natural theology" should be built upon facts concerning our moral and mental constitutions, as well as the mechanism of the material world. . . .

Since I decided to study for the ministry, I have received an offer of a somewhat attractive situation in a newspaper establishment, procured for me by an influential friend, to whom I had applied several months before. I was very sorry to disappoint him; but I could not avoid doing so without changing my plans of study, and repressing what I believe to be the promptings of duty.

My interest in the subject of my studies increases daily. In contemplating the glorious attributes of God, and in cherishing the proper notions of the dignity of human nature, I experience great and growing delight. I regret that I cannot be near you, and enjoy the pleasure and profit of frequent conversations; but perhaps the lesson of self-dependence will, in part, compensate for the privation.

May 18, 1849.

Since my return from Syracuse, I have studied regularly, with great enjoyment and profit. Mr. W. takes the *Christian Register*, and by exchanging with him I read both papers. I like the *Inquirer* best.

Its notices of the Anniversaries were capital, and more liberal than I had expected. What is said of the Meadville School is very proper. I suppose the comparison instituted between Meadville and Cambridge was intended to remove any jealousy which might exist among the friends of the latter, and not to directly assert that Meadville would furnish the privates, and Cambridge the officers, of the society. However, such matters will regulate themselves.

I am very much interested in the emancipation movement which is going on so bravely in Kentucky. When I read the proceedings of the late convention at Frankfort, I was overjoyed, for I thought that the South would yet be redeemed from the Slave Power which has so long crushed and disgraced her. I feel so much on the subject that if I had no other plans of duty, I think I should go to Kentucky and enlist in the army of Freedom.

June 9, 1849.

The Progressive Quakers have just closed their first yearly meeting. It was well attended, and they seem to be delighted with the result of their labors. Lucretia Mott, Oliver Johnson, and Joseph Dugdale of Ohio, were among the chief speakers. Among the addresses issued by the meeting is an excellent one "To Reformers," from the pen of Oliver Johnson. Mrs. Mott spoke to a large audience in the court-house, last Tuesday evening. She is a noble woman, and I think her discourse will aid the cause of Liberal Christianity in this vicinity.

Mr. W. has furnished me with tracts, which I have circulated among my friends, — some of whom read them willingly and attentively.

July 22, 1849.

I have six weeks more for reading before I start for Meadville. I continue to recite in Greek regularly.

You once asked me whether I wished you to procure for me the stipend which the American Unitarian Association allows indigent students for the ministry. After due deliberation, I have resolved not to ask for any such aid. I am well aware that a student is almost necessarily a *consumer*, when by engaging in other pursuits he might be a *producer* of money; and that if he is not rich, yet disposed to effect his education without foreign aid, he must practise self-denial and close economy; but, having a strong and almost romantic love of independence, while I have youth, health, and strength, I cannot consent to be the recipient of anything that looks like charity. If I err in this, the error is venial, for it springs from a dread of dependence and the servility which it so often breeds.

I read Dr. Bellows' letter, in which he speaks at great length of the Meadville School. His style is always animated and pleasing, and the information which he furnished was very interesting to me. Notwithstanding a different feeling on the first hasty reading, his representations make me more willing than ever to attend the institution.

I could not help smiling when I read the grave

remarks of certain " well-paid " clergymen who, at a
meeting in Boston during Anniversary week, mentioned one hundred and one hundred and fifty dollars
as ample incomes for men engaged in the work
for which the students at Meadville are preparing;
and my mirth was again provoked when I saw
Dr. ——'s complimentary allusion to the minister
on Long Island, who occupies the box of the stage-
coach in the week and the pulpit on Sunday. I
agree with the good divines when they pronounce
such men instruments of much good; but I have
no desire to engage in the profession under similar
circumstances. Dr. Dewey, in his article on the
" Pulpit," etc., expresses the true idea of what the
ministry is, and what it should be. If I am not
greatly deceived, the times now demand ministers
free from aristocratic tendencies and false notions
of refinement, and as far removed from coarseness,
ignorance, and vulgarity; men inspired with a sense
of the dignity and responsibility of their office, well-
informed on the great subjects of which they are to
speak, abounding in genuine delicacy and refinement,
and yet able to tolerate, appreciate, and in some
measure supply, the intellectual, moral, and spiritual
wants of all their hearers. I despise arrogance, fas-
tidiousness, and pedantry as cordially as I dislike
servility, vulgarity, and ignorance. The middle class
has ever been the best in society; and, desiring to
be one of its ministers, and believing that Meadville
affords the necessary means of preparation for such
a station, I shall attend the school gladly.

My friends, the Rev. Messrs. —— and ——, are very polite to me, but not quite as friendly as of old. Within a few months, Mr. —— has ceased to call me by the familiar title of "Thomas," substituting therefor "Mr. Mumford." Why the old gentleman has made this change, I cannot divine. He may mean to pay respect to "the cloth"; or he may think that in wandering from his flock and becoming a Unitarian I have *lost my Christian name.*

Mr. —— and I had a pleasant though spirited discussion of the doctrine of the Trinity, a few evenings since. He repeated the story about Dr. Channing's repentance and recantation, and, in reply to some of my remarks, impatiently exclaimed, " If the giant mind of *Newton* could implicitly receive this doctrine, it does not become *us* to talk about its reasonableness." Now, passing by his argument, which if valid is very weak, I wish to ask you if it was possible that I was in error when I replied that his example was extremely unfortunate, for Newton's Unitarianism is well-known. He very flatly, yet politely, contradicted this assertion. Since the conversation, I have noticed that Dr. Channing repeatedly claims Newton as a Unitarian; and in the " Encyclopædia Americana" and the "Cyclopædia of English Literature," I find statements which imply the same fact. Is there any doubt about Newton's faith ? . . .

The books you mention — De Wette, Herder, and the " Philosophical Miscellanies"—are very attractive. I long to read them, but dare not gratify my inclination at this time. I have reviewed almost every text-book which I have read, and have no great desire to go over them again at present; but my pride and dread of mortification prompt me to deny myself the reading of the books of my choice, and to apply myself for the next three weeks almost exclusively to the books upon which I am to be examined. I am confident that I now have a good knowledge of them; but, to avoid all slips of the memory, I suppose a general review is necessary.

IV

IN THE THEOLOGICAL SCHOOL.

Opinion of the School. — Fidelity to its Rules. — Hopes to be a Good Pastor. — Views of Non-Resistance. — First Attempt at Preaching. — Philanthropic Zeal. — Ill-Health. — Longs for Spiritual Culture. — Regard for Scandlin.

MEADVILLE, March 28, 1850.

My dear Friend,— You cannot imagine how much I have been benefited by your simple words of kindness and affection. I trust that I am moved to the discharge of duty by higher considerations; but words of cheer from a friend to whom I am so strongly attached incite me to renewed exertions, while they cause my heart to leap and sing for joy. I need not assure you that your feelings of kind regard are reciprocated.

I have now been in Meadville about twenty-nine weeks. I am satisfied that my sojourn has been, upon the whole, a pleasant and profitable one, and I trust I shall never repent it. My health has been uncommonly vigorous. I have won the confidence of several excellent friends, and I have pursued my studies with diligence. For several years before I left home I was accustomed to spend almost the whole day in uninterrupted study, and I apprehended some difficulty in adapting myself to the regular recitations of a school; but I have been agreeably disappointed. When I entered the institution, I resolved to discharge every known duty, and I confidently believe that that resolution has been kept most faithfully. Out of three hundred recitations which it has been my duty to attend, I have been absent from only one, and then I was unwell. I have never been late at any recitation. Out of one hundred and thirty chapel exercises, I have missed only one, and at that time a notice of a change in the hour had been misunderstood by me. Out of one hundred social meetings, debates, preachings by seniors, and lectures, I have missed but one, and at that time I was not well.

I was very glad to find the tone of the students, in respect to the great humanitary reforms which are the glory of our age, so healthy and active.

The school is really a moral oasis in the desert of a conservative community. In all his arduous and painful, yet heroic efforts for the sacred cause of humanity, Mr. Stebbins has the pleasing satisfaction of knowing that his pupils are, almost to a man, his devoted friends, admirers, and coadjutors.

My dear friend, I hope you will pardon me for yielding to the promptings of a full heart, and repeating expressions of affection and gratitude. Not a day passes in which I do not remember your kindness; and I fondly trust that when you become fully acquainted with me, you will find me not unworthy of your confidence and regard.

Hoping that God will bless you in all your relations and labors, and that you may be forever happy, I am your grateful and affectionate friend,

THOMAS J. MUMFORD.

MEADVILLE, May 18, 1850.

My dear Friend, — I know that you will be pleased to learn that the standard of Reform still floats from our school. Your remarks upon the duty of our nation and the sad apostasy of Daniel Webster delighted me. "You gave me my own thoughts."

Each day adds depth to the conviction that I shall be more useful and happier in the Christian ministry than I can be in any other sphere. I feel that I can give my whole soul to the work. Ever since I was a small boy, I aspired to be a public speaker, and all my reading and observation have been made to bear on the duties of such a vocation. But I think I shall succeed best as a *pastor*. I do love to hold intimate communion with the spirits of my fellow-men. I could find my highest joy in sympathizing with the poor and the suffering. I scout the idea that there is, or can be, any such being as an entirely hopeless and totally depraved sinner; and I think nothing could dishearten me if I were laboring to reclaim the abandoned. I have never found any difficulty in gaining the confidence of those with whom I have associated; and I know that I have aided a few of my unfortunate brethren by convincing them of my love, and by assisting in the resurrection of their self-respect.

On some subjects, where my mind has been held in suspense, I have come to decided opinions, since I last saw you; but I think that on only one important question have I had occasion to change. You may remember that I once told you that, while I condemned all ordinary wars, etc., I thought I could take life in defence of life, liberty, and chastity. I have reviewed Dymond with Mr. Stebbins, and I have been compelled to hold that nothing short of entire non-resistance will satisfy the Christian law. Resistance may sometimes appear to be clearly expedient; but I now hope that, should the hour of trial ever come to me, I may be able to act up to my conviction of duty, obeying implicitly the Divine law, and submitting cheerfully to every sacrifice, in the calm, firm trust that all will be well in the end,— that God will vindicate his own truth.

Of late I have had much pleasant intercourse with Mr. Stebbins. I think a conversation with him would be of great service to you, when you come to advise me about my future course.

We are great admirers of Horace Mann. How nobly has he rebuked Webster! Mr. Mann's style is apt to be too intense and over-emphatic; but his loyalty to truth and freedom is most refreshing in these degenerate days. I have predicted that he is soon to be Governor of Massachusetts, or to supersede the arch apostate in the Senate of the United States. I have been interested in the proceedings at the Anniversaries of the American Anti-Slavery Society. I was surprised, and deeply pained,

to hear of the success of the mob.   I blush for the
great city of our Empire State.   The Brooklynites
behaved nobly.   I think they were a little indiscreet
in befriending Wendell Phillips.   In one respect they
may find that, in their generosity, they have got
the Trojan horse within their walls.   He must be
rather a dangerous man for orthodox and conservative, but candid and virtuous, young men and women
to listen to.

WATERLOO, N.Y., July 3, 1850.

I have been urged to preach here, and some of my
acquaintances at Seneca Falls told me yesterday that
they would get up a meeting as soon as possible.   I
had made so many warm friends in Meadville that,
when I left on my vacation, it seemed almost like
going away from home.   I am very sorry to think
that Mr. Stebbins is to leave the school.   He is the
prince of professors and the idol of every student.

If I do not attend the convention, shall I come to
Syracuse the third Sunday in July?

Aug. 9, 1850.

I am glad to know that my services were accept-
able to your people.   I preached in Seneca Falls, last
Sunday afternoon.   The other churches had services at the same hour, but I had from one hundred
to one hundred and fifty hearers.   All seemed attentive, and several good Methodist brethren tarried to
thank me, and bid me Godspeed.   Next Sunday
evening, I shall preach here in the court-house.
We did not apply for any of the churches, thinking
it not best to trouble them to refuse.

My dear Friend, — Let me write to you on a subject which has occupied my thoughts much of late.
Love to God and love to man are the great precepts
of religion ; and they are generally said to be of
equal importance, to claim equal attention from the
minds and pens and tongues of true Christians. But,
to employ a figure of doubtful dignity, how few men,
how very few ministers, drive Piety and Philanthropy
abreast! Almost all drive them *tandem.* Most ministers put Piety "on the lead"; but a large and rapidly increasing class put Philanthropy first. I am
a little troubled because my own mind is so wont to
dwell on "moral" rather than "religious" subjects.
I cherish a sense of dependence on God, and a
cheerful trust in his providence. I feel the importance of always remembering that his eye is ever
upon us, that his "inclining ear" is ever ready to
hear our petitions; but I must confess that my
thoughts are devoted chiefly to mankind, to their
natures, duties, destinies. I felt called to the work
of the ministry by the pressing demand for more
abundant and faithful preaching of "peace on earth,
good-will to men." During the last fortnight, I have
often examined myself concerning my fitness for the
Christian ministry. I have faith in God. I love and
reverence Christ. The Christian religion is inex-
pressibly dear to me. My heart burns within me
when I read the memoirs of Channing and Follen,
and the Wares and Peabodys. I love my fellow-men.
I have no unkind feelings towards any human being.

I know that I am deeply concerned for the weak, the oppressed, the tempted, and the fallen. I long to lay bare the wrong which sin does to the soul, and to portray the beauties and joys of holiness. I am almost sure that neither wealth nor fame nor friendship could tempt me to sacrifice my integrity. I cherish a kind of spirit of martyrdom. I have a deep, earnest longing to spend and be spent in some good work, however unpromising and odious. I would rather go through this land in rags, "a hatless prophet," preaching needed truth kindly but boldly, than to be the well-paid pet of the most aristocratic society. My day-dreams and my visions of the night are of doing good to my fellow-men, especially to those whom the world despises and dreads. And when I sit down to write, "justification by faith," etc., etc., do not present themselves as candidates for my attention. And what is perhaps worst of all, while I know that I do not conform to the standard which so many erect for the Christian minister, my heart won't condemn me. I cannot persuade myself that I have mistaken the wants of the age, my own mission, and that of Liberal Christians generally. I cannot bring myself to believe that my position is at all deplorable. Do not misunderstand me. I would not slight devotion. I expect to preach a great many sermons on subjects strictly "religious." I only say that I feel called chiefly to another work,— to that of redeeming mankind from ignorance, sin, and misery. In short, I am probably too much inclined to be "nothing, if not practical."

March 6, 1851.

Our second term commenced about four weeks ago. During the winter vacation, I was quite unwell, having a very severe cold, and an increased noise in my head. I was confined to the house, and unable to read the simplest book with any satisfaction. My cold is gone, but my head is still the scene of a terrible commotion. I have attended all the exercises of my class, and applied myself to study more diligently than ever before, but I can accomplish little. In all my life, I have never suffered half so much in mind as during the last month. Sometimes my total defeat in repeated attempts to study has made me almost frantic. I suppose that even in my disabled condition, I can manage to drag through the exercises here and graduate next summer with the commendation of my teachers ; but I fear that in that event I shall not feel qualified to commence preaching regularly. I am at a loss what to do. My general health is not at all robust. The work of the ministry has grown upon me during the past year. I now see and feel that when I commenced my studies I had no adequate conception of its responsibilities, toils, and rewards. I have been gradually opening my eyes upon the sad religious insensibility of my own heart, and the hearts of the companions of my youth. I trust I now begin to realize the nature and importance of spiritual things and the interior life. On two accounts, therefore, — first, the state of my health ; second, to increase my heart preparation for the ministry, — I feel that it is better for me

not to enter the field this summer. I know that if
God blesses me with a return of health and strength,
in another year I can accomplish far more than I
have yet done. Can you give me any advice ? The
state of my head makes me very sad. I am very
anxious to determine upon some plan for the future.
My mind is now in a state of painful uncertainty.

March 21, 1851.

Since I wrote my last letter, my health has improved somewhat, although the sounds in my head
continue to torment me. I have resolved to remain
here, studying as well as I can, and graduate with
my class, in June. Mr. Stebbins thinks I had better
preach during the summer; and in the fall, if I feel
unable to undertake the work regularly without
further preparation, I can spend another year here,
or take some small society where I can have leisure
for study.

Within six months, I have had my eyes opened to
the greatness and glory of the work of a Christian
minister. It was with deep shame and sorrow that I
became convinced that my own standard had been
too low. I had been charmed by the ethics of the
gospel. I am earnestly seeking to know and feel
more of its spiritual power. James Freeman Clarke's
sermons have been of great service to me. I now
hope that I have commenced a truly religious life,
believing not only with the intellect, but with the
heart. However, I feel as if I needed to gain more
light and strength before I undertake to lead the

people. .... I was glad to see that glorious George Thompson received so glorious a welcome to Syracuse. It must have been a time of great satisfaction and joy for you all. How different from some of the scenes in which you were actors sixteen years ago! Such comparisons are more than mile-stones on the road to Truth.

April 6, 1851.

My very dear Friend and Father, — The reading of a letter from you *did* "cheer a gloomy moment," I can assure you. I wish I could half express the thrill of joy occasioned by the sight of your well-known superscription, and the lively pleasure I experienced in reading the words of kindness and sympathy which I knew your heart had promptly dictated, whether your pen had had leisure to record them or not. I thank you for them. They have done me much good, besides strengthening and deepening my affection for their author.

My health continues to improve steadily. The noises in my head are very loud, but since my mind has been more at ease I have suffered far less.

About a fortnight ago, Mr. Stebbins addressed me in the kindest manner, and told me not to permit fears of having to enter the ministry without sufficient preparation to make me unhappy. He said, "Go on with your studies as well as you can, graduate, and preach two or three months. Then, if your health is restored, and you feel as if you could not get along without a better preparation, come back and spend another year with us, renewing your

studies, and reading whatever may seem useful to
you." I thanked him, and have since felt much
relieved.

As I have written to you before, I have just had
my spiritual eyes couched, and begin to realize that
there is an "inner life," the glories of which I had
never imagined. But it will take me a long time to
change the current of my thoughts. Instead of
thinking of giving up the ministry, I have now a
desire to enter it far stronger than any I ever felt
before. I do feel that it is absolutely necessary for
me to devote more time to preparation than I had at
first intended. I must have more time to become
familiar with the Bible, and more time for spiritual
culture. I have no doubt I could begin to preach
this summer, and write *two things* which I might call
sermons; but they would consume all my time, and
utterly fail of making me contented. I fear that I
could not live "from hand to mouth" long, without
suffering from self-contempt and despondency. I
shall be very glad to preach a few months this
summer, if I have an opportunity; but I must postpone entering the regular service.

There are now in this school several young men
of the most unquestionable piety, with whom it is my
good fortune to be intimate. I must mention one in
particular, William Scandlin, a young Englishman,
lately of the United States ship "Ohio." He is preparing to be Father Taylor's successor, and, if I am
not mistaken, he will almost make the noble old
man's place good. Mr. Scandlin has been a sailor

ever since he was eight years old. You may have heard of his efforts on board the "Ohio" at the time so many of her crew died of yellow fever. He has a rich, deep voice, and a delivery which is almost unexceptionable. Then, too, he is so brave and active, yet gentle as a woman. His education is, of course, very limited; but he is a most diligent student, and learns rapidly. He is already a non-resistant, and much interested in the anti-slavery movement.

I am, as ever, your grateful and affectionate friend,

THOMAS J. MUMFORD.

Samuel J. May.

V.

LIFE IN DETROIT.

Leaves Meadville. — Character and Prospects of the Detroit Movement. — Frankness and Fidelity. — Extracts from First Sermons. — Anti-Slavery Sentiments. — Devotion to Mr. May. — Call and Ordination. — Remarks on Boston Ministers. — Missionary Work. — Building the New Church. — Unexpected Disaster. — Trip to Boston. Marriage. — Bereavement.

DETROIT, July 10, 1851.

My dear Friend, — On Wednesday of last week, I started for this place. Leaving Meadville was like leaving home. I had no idea that the beautiful village and its inhabitants had become so very dear to me, until the stage bore me up College Hill and I looked back upon the place. Notwithstanding my illness, and the misery occasioned by doubts of my fitness for my calling, I can now look back upon the scenes of the last two years with almost unalloyed pleasure. It is true that I have not made the progress in study which I had fondly hoped to make, but I know where to find knowledge, and that is something. I cannot tell you how happy all my social relations have been! Not an unkind thought, not an ungentle action, have I known. I never met a person who did not contribute to my happiness; and the manner of my teachers, fellow-students, and acquaintances assured me that their remembrance of me would be pleasant.

Our friends here meet in a very pleasant place, but it is an "upper room," in the third story, and rather long and narrow. Sunday morning, I had between seventy and eighty hearers; in the afternoon, about forty,—the usual attendance.

I am now at the house of the Treasurer of the Central Railroad Company. He is a very fine man, cultivated, cheerful, clear-minded, and large-hearted. Nine of the gentlemen connected with the society are employed in the railroad office. They all appear to be good men; they certainly are very busy. I find a great many old acquaintances here. Three or four families in the Unitarian Society are from Waterloo. Besides these, I have met a dozen gentlemen of other persuasions, whom I have known before. Several of them came to hear me, last Sunday.

I am endeavoring to cultivate my religious feelings more, but my interest in the great philanthropic movements is unabated. I fear that the people here are in favor of obeying the laws, however infernal they may be. Of course I shall not broach such subjects immediately; but before I accept an invitation to remain for any considerable length of time, I shall feel that simple honesty requires me to define my position. I do not want to be imprudent; I *cannot* be dumb. I feel pretty confident that a man like my host would despise a time-server. Indeed, all *men* would. All *men do* despise the poor contemptibles. At the same time I feel my own wants:

I need a more spiritual mind, and I must struggle to obtain it. That must be my chief concern at present.

July 21, 1851.

As I was coming up-stairs, just now, I remembered an old rule of health which I have heard you advocate: "Relax mind and body for an hour after dinner." There is no one near me with whom I care to be cosey, and I feel inclined to reply to your letter, even if my promptitude should seem amazing.

I need not repeat what I have so often said about your letters. They have, in times past, "made a sunshine in a shady place"; and now, when I am comparatively happy, they are doubly cheering.

I feel the force of your remark, that I shall only learn to minister *by ministering*, and I have duly pondered your other counsels. My health, and with it my spirits, continue to improve. I have been very agreeably disappointed in Detroit. It is a far handsomer place than I had supposed. I have seldom enjoyed a walk more than I did one to the cemetery, last evening. I think the people are interested in my services. They give me excellent attention, and I am frequently urged to make up my mind to settle here. The prospects of the society are quite encouraging. They tell me that between fifty and sixty gentlemen subscribe toward the support of the minister, and that others promise to do so as soon as it ceases to be an experiment. Very few persons have called on me, but they say it is not the fashion to visit the minister in this section. Wherever I go I receive the most cordial welcome. Everybody is very kind. And now that I have set forth the bright side, let me say something about the dark.

I find that they have never celebrated the Lord's Supper, and they seem disposed to postpone doing so until they shall have a place of their own. This is a cause of regret to me; for I covet the opportunity to impress others,— which the occasion affords,— and I need its influence myself.

There is very little interest in the reforms manifested in Detroit. The orthodox ministers advocate obedience to *the law*, and capital punishment. The press here is notoriously time-serving. Abuse of the abolitionists and sneers at the " Higher Law" are its favorite topics. In our society, I have discovered quite a number of men whose political views are of the Seward school. One of our trustees, however, made a handsome property while proprietor of a Cass organ, postmaster, etc. Thus far, I have had no occasion to allude to slavery, save in general terms ; but, of course, with my convictions, I cannot be always dumb. My organ of caution is a very large one, and I am not afraid of doing anything really rash ; but I am puzzled to know just what I ought to do. I am young, and so is the society ; and that fact ought to make us both modest. But, on the other hand, I cannot preserve my self-respect if I keep back needed truth, nor can any society be free from rottenness which is unwilling to bear it.

Again, I meet with wine and brandy whenever I enter society. The president of our society, a fine man, *with a family of boys*, has wine at dinner, and seemed a little surprised because I would not partake. The other evening, I was the only water-drinker in a circle of very clever people, — Episcopalians, Presbyterians, and Unitarians. Even the ladies seemed to fancy brandy and water! If I stay, they may depend upon it I shall "speak the truth in love."

P.S. — I have opened this letter, to tell you how interested I have been in considering your remark, that all that a Christian minister has to do is to preach what Christ preached, and live what Christ lived. For an hour past, I have not been able to think of anything else. I am satisfied that I can never become truly eloquent until I become as ardently attached to Jesus as Paul was. No! I don't mean that: I mean that my power to move men will be just in proportion to the depth of my love of Jesus, and my ability to manifest it. I feel that I ought to be as passionately fond of his teachings as some of my music-loving friends are of Jenny Lind's voice.

July 29, 1851.

I cannot help being filled with "righteous indignation" by the contemptible fling at you contained in this morning's *Advertiser*. The *Advertiser* is the leading Whig paper of this State. Of course you will laugh at it, and at me, perhaps, for sending it to you; but I wish to give you a faint idea of the meanness of the press hereabouts. I have never known such rotten concerns. The way in which they "come down" upon those "false teachers" who preach that "religion is higher than the State and the Constitution" is *a caution* to young ministers.

Thus far, I have avoided all allusions to the exciting topics of the day. My last text was, "Let us do good, as we have opportunity, unto all men." Among the ways of doing good *in the State*, I mentioned, "By helping to discountenance the demagogue and the political gambler; by aiding the election of good men of broad views and pure lives, who, instead of being mere partisans, will ever cast their vote and their influence into the scale of Justice, Truth, Peace, and Freedom. We may do good by elevating the standard of public morality, by seeing that religion *is* carried into politics, where it is so much needed, and kept there." While touching on "doing good in the Church," I said, "By endeavoring to have a Christian church an assembly of immortal souls, anxious to hear needed truth freely uttered,— not a society of pew-owners, gathered to have their ears pleased and their nerves composed by a 'chloroform gospel,' preached with elegance and 'decent debility'; not an association of men who are contented with formally professing, on a Sunday, to love their neighbor as themselves; but a real band of brothers, who are *pious. in plain clothes*, and whose week-days abound in deeds of self-sacrificing kindness."

I suffer much for the lack of society, but I welcome every trial in the way of discipline.

Mr. H.'s sister, from Cambridge, has just arrived. She is redolent of anti-slavery, and the sight of her is refreshing.

I was much amused, on Sunday. A shabbily-dressed man, who had listened eagerly to my sermon, called me aside as I was going "out of church," and complimenting the discourse, — the first he had ever heard from a Unitarian pulpit, etc., — finally gave me an "opportunity to do good" by paying for his dinner and supper. That was *practice* following pretty closely upon the heels of *preaching;* was it not?

In the evening, I was called upon to conduct funeral services at the house of a gentleman with whom I was unacquainted. The deceased was a lovely boy, eleven months old,— an only child. I spent several hours in careful preparation, and, when the time arrived, I obeyed Mr. Hosmer's injunction to "let the heart lead." A number of strangers were present. I was assured that my exertions had been blessed.

I am not acquainted with all the people yet. I hope I shall find my way to their hearts. I do not know what to think about being ordained an evangelist. If I determine upon that, I am at a loss to decide whether I shall visit Syracuse for that purpose, or try to have you come here. If you cannot come to me, I shall go to you; for I would rather wait a year than to have you absent.

Aug. 22, 1851.

For several weeks past my health has improved. Since I wrote last, I have visited Ann Arbor. I was frequently called upon to explain our views, and have been urged to return and give a public reply to the question, "What is Unitarianism?" I shall speak there next Sunday evening in the court-house. I am promised a large audience. I wish I had some tracts.

I think they will invite me to settle here, and I now feel inclined to accept, if my health holds out. If you are aware "of any just cause or impediment," I wish you would let me know immediately. I have not concealed my sympathy with the reforms of the day, nor my ideas of the independence of the pulpit. On that account a few may hesitate; but I am told that, so far as has been ascertained, there is an almost universal wish that I should stay.

I cannot tell you all the kindness of the H.'s to me. Mr. H. has treated me like a brother, beloved from the beginning. I spend many delightful hours in his house. It is my Detroit *home.* I am slowly getting acquainted with my people. I find that the minister is the bridge across many a social gulf. The people do not know each other, and I have no one to introduce me. I hunt them down singly.

On the first of August, I accompanied my colored brethren to Canada, crossing in a boat with about a hundred of them. "My heart leaped up when I beheld" several schools of the finest children the sun ever shone upon. Everything was done decently and in order, with no more parade than the whites make on their sham Fourth of July. I witnessed the laying of the corner-stone of a church. The ministers were all "colored," and to me the services were solemn in the extreme. They de-

posited copies of the *Liberator*, etc., in the box. I
was thrilled when I heard, " We consecrate this spot
to the worship of God our Father ; we consecrate
it to the defence of the rights and liberties of all men,
our brethren." I had no opportunity to tell them
publicly of my sympathy, but my heart and my eyes
were overflowing.

The recent kidnapping and murder in Buffalo!
Does not Christianity sometimes seem almost "a
failure"? I thank God it is not. My faith stands
the trial. Patience and earnest effort will yet cause
the right to triumph. When I see you, I must tell
you of a romantic idea of a new "company of Jesus,"
devoted to the overthrow of slavery, of which I
often dream

Sept. 3, 1851.

About ten days ago, the trustees of the society resolved to recommend me to the congregation. The
President and several others told me the vote was
unanimous and hearty. "Nobody thought of anything else." Last Sunday, I had about one hundred
and ten hearers,— the largest audience thus far. The
society then gave me a call by a vote as unanimous
and hearty as that of the trustees. They offered a
salary of $600. Besides that sum, their expenses are
at least $200 for rent, music, etc. The society has
been self-sustaining from the start, and they seem
to be in downright earnest. I shall accept, and
serve them to the utmost extent of the ability God
has given me.

As to "the practical reformatory tendencies of my faith," my conscience tells me I have done right. In private conversation with most of the leading men, and repeatedly from the pulpit, I have "defined my position" most distinctly. I have preached my sermon on "Speaking the Truth in Love," which you may remember. To be sure, I have not preached a sermon entirely devoted to any particular topic of reform, but my tendencies have been manifested abundantly. Many have assured me that no one can mistake my feelings and principles; they have appeared in almost every sermon and prayer. It may be that some will squirm yet when I preach directly at some partisan measure; but, from the moment I came here, I insisted that they should know my principles, and know also that they do not admit of compromise. I told them frankly that their society *might* suffer by their promulgation, urged them to remember that, when they should think of calling me, etc. Hereafter, no man can say he did not know that he was "catching a Tartar."

WATERLOO, Oct. 1, 1851.

I thank you for your suggestions concerning the place, etc., of the ordination. I, too, think that Detroit is the best place, even if we have to wait until next spring. I am becoming very fond of the pulpit. Every time I utter a noble sentiment, I seem to grow spiritually; for I preach to myself as well as to the audience.

I wished you to give me the charge, because I supposed that to be the most direct personal part of the services,—because I felt that injunctions from your lips would sink most deeply into my heart. If I have mistaken the nature of the services, if the sermon can be made as personal, I have no choice.

As I was leaving the pulpit, last Sunday evening, a former parishioner of yours came forward and told me she could not help expressing her delight, etc., and said it was in part owing to the fact that I reminded her of her old pastor every moment. Half-a-dozen people in Buffalo said, " How constantly you remind us of Mr. May! " Is it not singular? I have heard you only twice.

DETROIT, Oct. 17, 1851.

My dear Friend and Father,—Your kind, magnanimous letters came together, Saturday evening. I went to Mr. H. and Mr. W., and said, " I learn that the Eastern papers are abusing Mr. May, charging him with countenancing and assisting the rescue at Syracuse. I have just received a confidential letter to that effect. What shall I do? I want him to come. He has been more than a friend to me. He has ever manifested almost more than a father's interest in me, and I cannot reconcile myself to the thought of his absence. If he has become temporarily odious, never mind. I can cheerfully share his fate. If his coming would injure the prospects of our society,—oh! I will labor diligently to atone for it all. If the damages can be liquidated, take them out of the salary. I cannot give him up. Just think of Timothy's writing to Paul, telling him it was inexpedient for him to attend his ordination, as the chief priests and rulers in those parts called him a pestilent fellow and a mover of sedition!"

They seemed both amused and touched by my emotion, and said, "Tell him to come, by all means ; we don't believe he can do us any harm ; and what if he does?"

When the telegraph office-doors were opened, Monday morning, I entered with a message, urging you to come. I was assured that it would be sent immediately. I received no reply,—not even a letter. I have not heard from you since. I do hope nothing serious has occurred. When the "Mayflower" arrived, late Wednesday evening, I felt sure you were on board. I saw a man with a white hat. It was dark, and I rushed into his arms ; but it was not you! Imagine my disappointment when I learned you were not on board! But I soon concluded that you had endeavored to act for the best.

The ordination was postponed to Thursday evening. Mr. Hosmer preached to the congregation which had collected. Last evening, the services were all eloquent, excellent. J. F. Clarke's sermon was glorious,—true to God, true to humanity, as he always is. May God bless his dear soul!

Everything was excellent. But when, after the charge, I sat down and thought that you might be *in prison*, my emotions struggled hard for an expression which would have unfitted me for the remaining services; but God gave me strength to retain my self-possession.

I was touched by your son's unexpected kindness. I shall prize that mark of his affection most highly. God knows I love you all dearly. I have a thousand thoughts I cannot utter now.

Your friend and son,

T. J. M.

Nov. 6, 1851.

My very dear Friend and Father,— Your favor of the 2d inst. has just reached me. I was delighted to get it. I read it in the street, and became so absorbed as to narrowly escape capsizing several fellow-citizens, who did not observe that I was engaged. I knew how you must have felt concerning the ordination; still, I could not help being sorely disappointed. You can scarcely imagine how my heart yearned for the charge; and you would be astonished, could you realize how many ardent friends you have among my little flock. I am proud of my people because they were so willing to have you come, in spite of the popular prejudice. With almost maternal partiality, I almost believe there never were such parishioners.

I cannot think that the administration are so blind and mad as to hasten their destruction by arresting you. I confess, I wish they would. I don't want to hear that you are hanged, and I don't expect to; but I think exceptions may be taken to the old maxim, "You can put a man to no worse use than to hang him." It depends upon what you hang him for. I have great faith in the utility of martyrs. Is not their blood the seed of the Church? If I know my own heart, I would most joyfully meet imprisonment, and death itself, rather than obey the Fugitive Slave Law, or even refrain from pronouncing it damnable.

I shall suffer, if you suffer; indeed, it would be wrong for me, young, without a family, son of a slave-holder, too, to stand by, preaching the gospel generally, while one in your relations is losing all the things of time for the sake of the slave.

I thank you for your suggestion respecting connected sermons. My plan is to have one discourse of each Sunday a "regular,"— the other of the "Guerilla" stamp. I never write a sermon without wishing I could read it to you. I have just finished one on the True Church. I speak first of the Church of God, of which the Church of Christ is a branch. In it I find the good Samaritan, Pontiac the great Indian, and other worthies.

"This Church of God is the only universal one. To the human eye it seems unorganized. It exists everywhere. Its origin may be dated back before the time of righteous Abel. Its end will never come: for, like all things truly good and great, it is eternal. Who are members of this Church? All who, in any age, in any country, under any form of faith, have loved truth and reverenced right, doing good and living beautiful and holy lives, whether they called the Deity ' Jehovah, Jove, or Lord '; whether they worshipped under roofs of man's erection, in the great church of Nature, that —

> "'Cathedral, boundless as our wonder,
> Whose quenchless lamps the sun and moon supply;
> Its choir, the winds and waves; its organ, thunder;
> Its dome the sky,'

or in that best of oratorics, on the most sacred of altars, the inmost recesses of a pure heart."

Nov. 18, 1851.

Last Sunday forenoon, my text was, Our *Father;* in the afternoon, *Our* Father, — my best sermons thus far, I think. At all events, they elicited much feeling and many hearty thanks from my best hearers. In the evening, I was a little frightened. They seemed about to applaud audibly. Let me copy a passage or two, to show you on what food I try to keep alive the spirits of my people. I will select passages good in sentiment rather than rhetoric.

"Christianity does not consist in a proud priest-hood, a costly church, an imposing ritual, a fashionable throng, a pealing organ, loud responses to the creed, and reiterated expressions of reverence for the *name* of Christ, but in the *spirit* that was in Jesus, the spirit of filial trust in God, and ardent, impartial, overflowing love to man. If there is in the whole universe of God a human being whose wrongs we regard with indifference, whose failings or deformities or degradation we view with cruel scorn, whom in any way we neglect and despise, we are not truly

Christians; nor are we even pious. I care not how frequent may be our devotions, nor how sound our faith, nor how profuse our offerings to God; though we spend our days in prayer, and our nightly visions are of heaven; though our belief is free from the slightest taint of heresy; though every church in the land is vocal with praises of our generosity, and every religious paper filled with tributes to our piety,—if we can look with criminal coldness upon the wrongs of even the least of Christ's brethren, we are not lovers of God. . . .

" There is another way of slighting humanity, of which I wish to speak,—in the common, almost universal belief that some professions are of superior dignity; that the seat of honor or reverence lies, not in the man, but in his calling. This error cannot be rebuked too frequently or too pointedly. It is the parent of much of human pride and jealousy. Many of our titles are absurd, and it requires some patience not to be restive under them. There are scores of members of Parliament, Congress, and Assembly to whom as little honor is due as to any being born of woman. There are many clergymen who should be treated with irreverence, if their abused humanity did not exempt them from the indignity; and, on the other hand, are there not obscure men and women who deserve our profoundest esteem and homage? Who has not known 'Most Honorable' farmers, 'Right Reverend' mechanics? Let every man rise or fall with his own individual character. A *man* is a nobler title than that of hero, priest, or king. . . .

"It seems eminently the duty of an American
to be philanthropic,— to cherish human rights, to
denounce earnestly and eloquently human wrongs.
Our country professes to be the chosen home, the
peculiar abode, of humanity and equality. To our
shores hundreds of thousands of the natives of
Europe come every year. At this moment, from the
President to the poorest vagrant in our streets, we
are all anxiously awaiting the arrival of the greatest
of modern martial heroes, with whose noble defence
of the liberties of his country 'all Europe rings
from side to side.' But are we truly consistent? Is
not our reverence for humanity partial? Does it
not depend upon accidents rather than essentials?
Do we not ourselves tolerate wrongs which shame
the friends of freedom throughout the world?"

Jan. 26, 1852.

It is just three years, this week, perhaps this day,
since I got into the cars at Waterloo and rode with
you to Auburn; and now here I am, busy and happy,
with a rapidly increasing society, and rich in my
first fifty sermons! My society comes on nicely, the
morning audiences having increased from seventy
to a hundred, and the evening from thirty-five to
seventy-five. My people are not rich, but honest
and generous. My salary is paid promptly; and the
treasurer assures me that the people pay it most
cheerfully, with many kind words by way of accom-
paniment. I have continued to utter my sentiments
on every subject in a frank, manly way, and have

given no offence even when I anticipated it. All my relations are delightful, and I am very happy. The only drawback to my bliss is the fear that I have entered the field prematurely, without taking time enough for preparatory studies. I hope to exchange with Shippen, in March. One exchange in five months is not too much for one who has hardly covered the bottom of his barrel with sermons.

I am much delighted with Kossuth. His reply to Chancellor Walworth was prompt and noble.

I expect to attend the Boston Anniversaries. You know I have not seen half-a-dozen of my New England brethren. I wish to hear Parker, King, Gannett, Huntington, and Pierpont. I want to see Federal Street Church and Faneuil Hall. I wish also to go on a pilgrimage to Amesbury. Mr. Whittier's poems wrought my "change of heart" on the subject of slavery.

I wish I could see you once a week. It is very hard to be so isolated in the first year of one's ministry. I am often lonely. But I am well aware of the numerous and pressing demands which are made upon your time, and therefore your silence never pains me. Whenever you are able to write, I am the most grateful of Timothys.

Your grateful and affectionate son,

T. J. Mumford.

June 17, 1852.

We have not commenced our church, but it will go up very soon. Our lot is a fine one, high, central, yet retired. We hope to pay for the church ourselves. Our society has never received a cent from abroad, and I think we shall not solicit anything hereafter.

From what I saw of New England ministers, at Cincinnati, I must say that my desire to visit Boston has greatly abated, and I do not know what would tempt me to go there asking funds for our church.

Dr. —— spent a night here, last week, leaving on Saturday morning for the East. I did not see him. Mr. —— asked him to stay and preach for us, but he did not seem at all inclined to do so. He went to Buffalo, where there is a strong society needing no help, a regular church, an organ, a gown, and all the other essentials of the Christian ministry.

In Cincinnati, Dr. —— and Mr. —— made me very indignant by their anecdotes, calculated, and apparently designed, to ridicule Dr. Channing's tone and manner and his complaints of ill-health.

Our politicians are looking anxiously towards Baltimore for the Whig nominations. I hope Fillmore will be the man; not because I admire him,— heaven deliver me from that!— but because, supported as he is by the whole South, his nomination will hasten that glorious day when present political organizations shall be blown to atoms, and the great party of freedom shall rally and triumph!

Is it true that Wm. Henry Channing is coming to Rochester? I hope it is, for I long to meet him. He is one of my idols.

May 31, 1852.

From Cincinnati, I went to Meadville. I found that I could not afford to attend the Boston anniversaries. I am sorry you could not attend the Western Convention. You were missed, I can assure you. The anti-slavery folks could hardly be reconciled to your absence. James Freeman Clarke is coming to inquire about the condition of the fugitives here. I hope you will meet him. He is very much interested in their cause.

I am glad the prospects of your church are so good. Our friends here think of building, this summer. They have purchased a fine lot.

June 17, 1852.

I wish I could be here to go into Canada with you. It does not cost much to visit the land of the fugitives. If you wish to visit Amherstburgh, or Malden, as it is called, the place where " George " and " Eliza " landed, the " Arrow," probably the very boat which transported Mrs. Stowe's heroine, will take you there, in about an hour, for a few shillings. I am told that the officers of this fine little boat never fail to land on the Canada shore, business or no business, if there are promising-looking colored men on board.

July 5, 1852.

It is noon, and they are firing cannon almost under my window. This fact must excuse some of my hieroglyphics.

Yesterday was the "Glorious Fourth!" My texts were, "If I forget thee, O Jerusalem!" etc., and,

" Righteousness exalteth a nation." I do love my country most fondly, and I have never been convinced that the Union is not a great blessing. I was pretty patriotic in the first half of the discourse, and when I came to slavery, I spoke ten minutes as distinctly and emphatically as possible, yet with kindness. I had a full house, one-third strangers. After service, the trustees had a meeting. We have only $7,000. Our lot cost $3,000. If we had only to provide for ourselves, we could get along nicely; but it will never do to build a small or shabby house in this beautiful, growing city. We have a fine plan for a house, but it will cost $8,000 or $9,000. The trustees feel determined to build, and to build according to the plan. No one ever dreams of foreign aid. I cannot help thanking God for that. I have no doubt the money will be raised and the building begun by the time you come. I do not believe that any man ever spoke to a more kind, considerate, generous assembly than the one that gathers in the Hall. Oh, how I love them! I am interested in their business, their families, their souls, their everything.

But I must go away from this tremendous firing. Give unto all thine household the warmest love of thy son,   TIMOTHY.

P.S. — My most intimate friend, U. Tracy Howe, will deliver the address before the literary societies of our State University, on the 20th inst. I am very, very sorry to be absent. You must go with him.

Ann Arbor is a beautiful village. I spoke there, last evening; court-house full. I never had a more attentive audience, and the stock of tracts did not begin to supply the demand. I am very anxious that you should know Mr. Howe. He is one of Nature's noblemen, and my love for him almost passes that of woman. Again, farewell.

THE "MAYFLOWER," Sept. 26, 1852.

I am now on my way to Meadville, to make my last visit for the year 1852. I expect to have a very pleasant time ; indeed, I am going "on purpose." I shall return, in about ten days.

Sunday before last, Mr. Howe read aloud Parker's grand sermon at the Simms anniversary. He did it justice, and I was frequently reminded of your remark of Parker, "In morals he is *tremendous.*" That's the word.

I have been much gratified and entertained by the impression which you made upon different members of my flock. All who heard you seem to have been highly pleased. Some were surprised to see so quiet a fanatic, so cool an incendiary. Mrs. S. has become an admirer of yours. I do not suppose she ever encountered a genuine ultra-reformer before, and you have relieved her mind of some painful dread of the class. . . .

Until about a month ago, I felt a little impatient because our church did not begin to go up; but now I am perfectly satisfied. It is ascending briskly, and will be enclosed in very good season. As the winter approaches, the attendance begins to increase. Within a short time, I have learned several facts about members of my flock which have encouraged me greatly.

Last evening, I completed my engagement at Ann Arbor. I have spoken there eight times to audiences ranging from thirty to three hundred. I must confess, however, that the smallest congregations have been the last two; but I attribute this in part to a satisfied curiosity, the efforts of the Orthodox, and rival meetings at the same hour, and in part to the nights being dark and stormy, and the cars keeping me an hour behind my usual time.

Oct. 11, 1852.

When will your church be dedicated? I hope to see ours enclosed in a few weeks. They commence the brick-work to-day.

Nov. 6, 1852.

Our church will be ready for the roof next week. Mrs. S. was here last Sunday, and heard me speak of Daniel Webster. I spoke kindly, yet most distinctly, of his private and public iniquities. Poor man, how I pitied him! Retribution is seldom so prompt!

P.S. — Monday morning. I have just time to add that we had a very high wind before daylight, yesterday morning, which blew down the west wall of our church, breaking the beams for the floors, etc., etc. It is quite a blow to us. The church was just ready for the roof, and the season is almost gone. *We* are not cast down.

BOSTON, Dec. 17, 1852.

This is my fifth week in Boston. They have been weeks of mingled enjoyment and suffering. The latter, however, has greatly predominated. Begging is not my forte, and never was a poor fellow in a state of greater agony. I cannot tell you of the coldness and rebuffs which I have received, nor of the kindness which some have manifested. Perhaps after it is all over I shall feel better and more grateful.

I have now secured $600 in Boston, and $100 in Concord. I hope to increase the sum obtained here to $1,000. Then I shall go to New Bedford, Salem, Providence, Worcester, and New York, hoping to pick up a few hundreds on my way home.

I look forward to several years of self-denial, hard work, and single-wretchedness with a struggling society. It will take a thousand dollars to put us where we were before the calamity overtook us. But I am a little too much prone to overrate the difficulties in my way. If I am disappointed, I generally manage to be pleasantly disappointed. Our church has gone up again, and I suppose the roof is on again by this time.

DETROIT, July 29, 1853.

Since my return, I have been overwhelmed with duties and calls of business and congratulation.*

* Married in Meadville, Pa., June 23, 1853, Thomas James Mumford and Sarah Yates Shippen.

Our church will be dedicated on Thursday, the 8th of September, and we shall be very happy to see you at the services. Mr. Stebbins is to preach the sermon, and we hope for quite a goodly attendance of the brethren from abroad. Everything continues to go on smoothly. Our church is much admired, and I hear many flattering predictions of a large congregation in a few years.

The sentiment of filial affection and gratitude, as I am assured, is shared by Sarah, the wife of your son,   TIMOTHY.

May 31, 1854.

Monday was a day of terrible suspense to us. . . . Yesterday afternoon, I buried the little boy, whom we had named for our Chicago brother, in our beautiful cemetery at Elmwood. At the grave, I recited these lines : —

> "To the Father's love we trust
> That which was enshrined in dust;
> While we give the earth to earth,
> Finds the soul its heavenly birth;
> Angels wait the angel-child,
> Gentle, young, and undefiled.
>
> "Give the spirit, then, to God,
> And its vesture to the sod;
> Life, henceforth, shall have a ray
> Kindled ne'er to pass away,
> And a light from angel eyes
> Draws us upward to the skies."

My grief at the loss of the child was almost swallowed up in joy for its mother's safety. . . .

We had a fine time at Louisville. Judge Pirtle's report came up, and I made a pretty earnest speech. I said that the reason given for defining our position with respect to the miracles, *viz.:* "Whereas there is a misunderstanding of the views of Unitarians," etc., etc., proved altogether too much; for our views are misunderstood on every subject. After threatening to move that the report be referred back to the committee, with instructions to amend by defining our position on all the subjects in systematic theology and practical Christianity, with particular attention to inspiration and retribution and war and intemperance and slavery, I said something like this:

"While I am willing to admit that my religious sensibilities have been deeply wounded by some of the words of Mr. Parker, I am unwilling to have it appear that we consider his the most dangerous infidelity. The worst scepticism in America has not been heard in the Music Hall, at Boston, but in these Christian churches, many of them unquestionably orthodox, whose ministers have preached that an infamous human law, which commands us to increase heavy burdens, and not to let the oppressed go free,—a law commanding injustice and hating mercy, —is binding upon our consciences. Mr. Parker may reject Christ. These men certainly dethrone God."

Judge Pirtle's report is to be printed, accompanied by a disclaimer of all indorsements by the Conference.

I found many Kentucky women who responded warmly to my anti-slavery talk. Some of them over-

whelmed me with sympathy. I am anxious to hear
the end of the Boston slave case. Syracuse seems
to keep the old fires burning.

Dec. 22, 1854.

The infant church at Detroit is now able to walk
alone nicely. We have about sixty members of the
church proper. Nearly eighty of our pews are occupied, yielding an income of about $1,600. The min-
ister's salary is now a thousand dollars, and, during
the year that is closing, he has received presents
amounting to half as much more. Our Thanks-
giving collection for the poor was much larger than
that of any of the wealthy societies of the city.
Believing in the concentration of effort, I am aiming
at the establishment of a ministry-at-large, to be
started next year, if possible. To this work, I shall
give my best energies for some time.

Each year greater importance is conceded to our
society, and I am treated with increasing courtesy.
I do not, however, purchase peace by concealment of
differences. While I aim to be truly evangelical, I
give no quarter to Calvinism, in any of its more or
less horrible forms. We are trimming our church
for Christmas, and hope to have a good celebration.

Oct. 19, 1855.

Your favor of the 17th inst. has just been received,
and I thank you with a full heart for its words of
sympathy and cheer. I wish we *could* sit side by
side for a few hours ; for, in this season of loneliness,
I often turn with new interest to the friends whom I

have long known and loved. You will be glad to know that I am generally calm and cheerful. Of course there are days when I am very sad; but the last hours of my wife were beautiful beyond description, and by new devotion to the work given me to do I hope to shorten the time of separation and heighten the bliss of reunion. The day is dark and cloudy, but, in the universe of a good Father, "At the evening-time it shall be light."*

April 7, 1856.

I am quite well, and busy according to my spirits and strength. My pulpit has never been cared for so faithfully as during the last six months. In December, January, and February my church was literally full; but with the approach of warm weather the congregation diminishes somewhat. Yesterday morning my sermon was on "The Attractions of the Ministry." I feel that no preacher discharges the debt due to his profession until he has confirmed the choice of some youth whose voice shall be lifted up for practical righteousness, when that of his elder brother in the ministry shall be hushed in death. By the way, I suspect that my love for you has always had a great deal to do with my love for the ministerial calling. Very few men could have impressed me so favorably on a first acquaintance. I shall never forget how ardently I have longed for the time when I should be a co-worker with Jesus and with you in the redemption of mankind from ignorance, sin, and misery.

* Died in Meadville, Pa., Sept. 24, 1855, Sarah, wife of Thomas J. Mumford.

June 5, 1856.

I was delighted to learn that your illness had been exaggerated. May you still have many years of strength and hope, to befriend the noble causes to which you are devoted, and to cheer the legion of friends who love you!

Of course I have been very much excited by the outrage at Washington and in Kansas. The assault upon Sumner came right home to my own heart; for if I have any idol among our public men it is Charles Sumner. For the last nine years I have read everything that he has published with exceeding satisfaction and delight. My sermon on " The Reign of Ruffianism in the United States," was well received. There are a few Hunkers in my congregation, but I rejoice to know that a large majority wish to hear the great gospel of human freedom distinctly and earnestly preached.

I hope you will get to Chicago. You have hardly had an opportunity to learn the spirit of our Western brethren. We have our alloy of conservatism, but Conant, Shippen, Murray, Staples, Moulton, Kelsey, and several others, are of the advance party in theology and reforms. Huntingtonism would be the death of Liberal Christianity in the West, and I am glad to see that even in New England the reaction has apparently commenced.

Nov. 4, 1856.

At last the great day has come, and I am hoping and praying that it will prove to be " the day of the Lord."

While at the polls, I overheard a good remark. A master blacksmith, six feet four inches in height, famous for his great physical strength and his big, kind heart, but by no means " hopefully pious," was talking to a Republican who belongs to a Presbyterian church whose minister denounces Sumner and Beecher. I heard him say, " Mr. ——, if there is anything that makes me sick of religion, it's that —— Border Ruffian pulpit of yourn!!" Of course that's profane language ; but it does not grate on my ears half so harshly as the prayers of a Rev. Cream Cheese.

Thanks for the *Liberators* containing your letter to II. C. Wright. I liked it exceedingly, just as I do everything that you say and do, my dear father.

I " shrieked for freedom" again, last Sunday. One man has left my church, and a few more are troubled by my words ; but I thank God that the most of my .people like to hear their watchman blow the trumpet of Righteousness and Truth. I have reason to know that my words disturb the greatest pro-slavery magnates in the State, and I rejoice to know that they *are* disturbed thereby. Out of thirty ministers, there are only four who speak for liberty. Dr. —— is defending the Mosaic account of the Creation, in a course of lectures ; and Mr. —— is interpreting the book of Revelations : but, between this Alpha and this Omega, there are some good words uttered for the weightier matters of the law by Congregationalist, Baptist, and Covenanter.

For the sake of Kansas, I hope Fremont will be elected; but I am not sure that the choice of Buchanan would not hasten the "good time coming" when, in peace or war, by vote or sword, the oligarchy of Satan will be utterly overthrown.

Aug. 6, 1857.

The time fixed for the meeting of our Ministerial Association is the week before the autumnal Convention. It seems, therefore, that, unless you care to take two Western excursions, you will be obliged to choose between the Jerry rescue and the meeting at Jefferson. Without intending the least disrespect for the memory of Jerry, or the slightest indifference to the merits of his saviours, I think you will be wise to prefer the gathering in the Western Reserve. It is a noble region, because it is inhabited by noble men. Indeed, if there is any "Holy Land" on this hemisphere, it is North-eastern Ohio, where there is no occasion for rescuing a man from the hands of his oppressors ; for no man-stealer ever dares on that soil to *claim* God's children as property. You cannot help being perfectly delighted with the love of universal freedom which animates the souls of Giddings' constituents, and I hope you will not lose this opportunity to speak to them.

Feb. 13, 1860.

To-morrow is St. Valentine's day ; but, as I do not feel disposed to wait any longer, I shall send you my love-letter *now.* Perhaps it will reach Syracuse at the appropriate time.

Your concern about my health is not altogether unreasonable, and still I feel bound to continue to do pretty much as I have done since I came home. Out of twenty sermons that I have preached, nineteen have been new ones; but the labor of preparing them has not been so exhausting as anxiety lest they should fail to interest the people after they were ready. Thus far, however, there has been no lack of encouragement. The great majority of the people, including all the "old guard" who have been here for years, are firm friends of mine, and as willing to have me spare myself as you yourself can be. Many of my very best parishioners, however, have moved away, and those who are in their places "know not Joseph."

Although I received not a dollar from my society the year that I was absent, the current expenses exceeded the income between seven and nine hundred dollars; so that this year we must raise nearly three times as much as was raised last, if we are to escape indebtedness. While I was away, one of our largest contributors lost his interest in the services, and moved a little way out of town; and now it is difficult to revive his willingness to do and give. The other churches of the city are provided with abler preachers than they ever had before, and they are more cordial to strangers than I can induce my people to be. Still, there is a disposition to be more active, our congregations are good, and more than half of the debt has been paid by subscriptions and extra assessments of the pews. If I had a little more strength and hope, I could fight it through ; and I am disposed to try it, as it is.

My family have never seemed so dear to me, and there are at least a few friends in Detroit to whom I am most devotedly attached. If I die first, I shall wish them near me at the last of earth ; and, if they go before me, I wish to pay the tribute to their worth that cannot be as well said by any other lips.

The constant hurry and drain of this outpost have prevented my acquiring that scholastic style which is preferred in New England, and it would be as easy to work on after the old fashion here as to learn new modes of thinking and writing elsewhere.

Your playful proposition of a barter of churches is decidedly complimentary to me; but I should not dare to undertake to fill your place for any length of time, and your people will not allow you to leave them again.

I go to the gymnasium, and my strength increases. If I could get rid of dissatisfaction with myself, and be contented with doing what I can, I should get along very well ; but I am too much beset by concern lest my duties to God and men are imperfectly performed. I need to be "justified by faith," forgetting the works of the law.

MEADVILLE, July 7, 1860.

I ought to have written to you some time ago, to relieve some of the fears naturally excited by my lugubrious communication. The troubles in my head probably remain about the same ; but the rest of the last month, the pleasing excitements at Quincy and this dear place have caused me to feel temporarily better. When I resume my labors, I intend to try a vesper service, with extemporaneous remarks; and, if that does not prove satisfactory, I must quit my post. I came away from Detroit leaving my people in the best of spirits on account of the success of our first " Festival and Fair." Although hastily prepared for, it yielded more than five hundred dollars clear profit. This finishes wiping out the debt which I found awaiting me when I got back from New England.

MEADVILLE, Oct. 27, 1860.

I am glad you approve the step that I have felt obliged to take. Already I begin to breathe " freer and deeper." A year or two at Marietta will probably restore me to my full vigor, and I shall not be astonished to find myself stronger than I have ever been before.

I felt drawn to this place to see Edgar Huidekoper, who is to spend the winter at the South, and may never return. He is one of my truest and most devoted friends. How I do thank God for the love of the noble that he has vouchsafed to give me! It makes me feel richer than Astor to count over the heavenly treasures that can be taken out of this world.

DETROIT, Nov. 19, 1860.

It is very hard leaving Detroit. I had full confidence in the general affection of my people, but I did not realize that *all* of them loved me so much, nor that I had so many friends outside of my church. I leave the society in very fair condition, and go away without an enemy, I believe, and hardly a lukewarm friend.   How can I be sufficiently grateful for all this affection !

VI.

AT MARIETTA.

Letters on the War. — Forecast of the Future. — Interesting Reminiscences of Early Life in the South. — A Scare at Marietta. — Second Marriage.

MARIETTA, Jan. 25, 1862.

How the war drags! Sometimes I have grave fears arising out of the timidity of the Administration, and the inevitable complaints that will attend the first attempt to enforce direct taxation. You know the Constitution distributes such taxes according to *population*. Already the Western papers are raising the cry that in fairness it must be according to *wealth*.

There are a few promising omens. War with England is at least postponed. There is reason to hope for a general pressure upon the rebels, from all quarters, if McClellan ever recovers from his *slow fever*. The new Secretary begins well. Burnside is trustworthy. The country is cheered by news of a victory in Kentucky, Cheever is tolerated at Washington, and Charles Sumner has become the leader of the American Senate! I extract comfort from this dilemma: If we have an early and easy success, the war will be over, and in the national pillion the Slave Power will hereafter ride behind; if the strife is prolonged and desperate, there will be no Slave Power left at the end of the struggle.

Feb. 20, 1862

I have just seen Parker Pillsbury's letter in the last *Anti-Slavery Standard*, which tells of your severe illness at Albany. From his mention of your illness, I am encouraged to believe that, if violent, it may have been a brief attack.

You wrote before our recent victories, and still your tone was very hopeful. You appeared to be confident that the Slave Power is soon to be crushed, and thousands of the slave-holders banished from the country. I am writing just after much cheering news, and yet I cannot rid myself of the apprehension that the anti-slavery cause may not have seen its worst days in our land. I dread the consequences of the easy triumph that seems to be at hand. If we continue to prevail, the end of strife must be near. Suppose the Southerners are shrewd enough to surrender the moment their cause becomes hopeless, and, professing regret for past errors, offer to return to the old Constitution and Union. In the reign of "good feeling" that will come with peace they will not receive very harsh treatment at the hands of such men as Lincoln and Seward. Then may come a war with England, in which our present division may be forgotten for several years. Then will come the next Presidential election. Let the restored South unite as of old with Northern Democrats who can charge the corruptions of the war upon the Administration, and thus win many votes from a heavily-taxed people, and once more the Slave Power leaps into the saddle, with sharpened spurs on its heels and a new cracker on the lash that has scourged all opponents of the Fugitive Slave Law. The pro-slavery Democrats have at least their share of the heroes of this war. The first Congress after our peace will be full of them. God knows that in spite of my love for a few individuals at the South, I would not murmur if the fate of Tories should be visited on slave-holders; but I think the heavy hand of the United States Government is just as likely to strike down Garrison and lock up Phillips. Of course, the final doom of slavery is certain; but it may yet be powerful enough to control this generation of Englishmen and Americans. This is a dark, damp day. I have been much elated by the success at Fort Donelson. Perhaps I am writing under the influence of the reaction of feeling that follows intense excitement. I shall be glad to find that you are by far the better prophet. . . .

You may be interested in the fact that the scene of the bombardment at Port Royal is not far from my native place. I was born at Gillisonville, about thirty miles from Beaufort. During his stay at the South, my father was postmaster at Coosawhatchie and at Pocataligo. His store was at Coosawhatchie, and he became intimately acquainted with many leading men, including Mr. Rhett, then named Barnwell, Mr. Petigru, the best lawyer in the State and almost the only consistent Unionist, and Henry Bailey, who was the Attorney-General who warned Mr. Hoar to leave Charleston. Mr. Bailey died before my father,

I think, and I remember destroying a large bundle
of his letters which I had read with intense interest.
I am quite sure that the Goddard Bailey who stole
the respectable sum of $800 worth of bonds from
the United States Government was his son, and
sometimes my playmate. Mr. Colcock, Collector
of the Port of Charleston, and formerly member of
Congress, was my father's lawyer ; and once, ten or
twelve years ago, when mother was in want of ready
money, he sent her a large draft to pay a very old
claim that he had chanced to collect. He refused
all compensation for his services in the matter.
Father was once toasted at a dinner in Beaufort
District as "Mumford — the honest Yankee." It
was intended for a compliment, but he felt the blow
at the North that it implied. Anticipating a col-
lision at an earlier day than it has occurred, he disposed of his property after the Nullification troubles,
and returned to Rhode Island. Mother left the
South with great reluctance. Indeed, it almost broke
her heart. Now, however, she is glad that we came.
About eight years since, she spent a winter with
some of our cousins in the old neighborhood, but she
had no desire to remain permanently.

While I appreciate their follies and sins, my heart
persists in tender memories of the kindnesses of some
of those planters, and I often wonder how they are
faring in these terrible days. On one plantation
where they love us still, a mother and two unmarried
daughters live with sixty or seventy slaves, and only
an overseer for their guardian. My father never

owned more than six slaves at a time, keeping just enough for house servants. When we were there, Coosawhatchie had the Court House, but now it is at Gillisonville. Those towns are all villages of the slenderest populations.

July 8, 1862.

You saw our watchword at the Detroit Conference, "Mercy for the South; Death to Slavery!" I wish you could have been there. Every voice was cordially for freedom.

I am to leave Marietta in a few weeks. My stay here has been delightful to me. My relations to the society of Unitarians have been as agreeable as possible, and all denominations, including the Catholics, have treated me with great kindness. But the climate is too enervating. If I am ever to be strong, I must spend some time in a more bracing air. So I am going to live at Groton, Mass., for a year, at the home of my wife's * mother. Of course you will come to see us. We will give you a room from which you may see Wachusett and Monadnock at one look.

Sometimes the war weighs heavily on my heart, but God is so evidently dealing with us that I have few permanent fears. Our weather is terribly hot. I pity the wounded who cannot get air and ice.

* Married in Groton, Mass., Aug. 27, 1861, Thomas James Mumford and Elizabeth Goodrich Warren.

VII.

REMOVAL TO NEW ENGLAND.

Birth of his Son. — *At Concord, Yonkers, Groton, and Green-field.* — *Death of his Mother.* — *Call to Dorchester.*

MARIETTA, July 30, 1862.

Yesterday noon we heard that the rebels were attacking Parkersburg in strong force. The Mayor of Parkersburg sent for help to our mayor. Marietta was aroused. Companies were formed,—one to go to Parkersburg immediately. Horsemen were sent to alarm the country towns. Reinforcements were asked from Athens. Then came another message from Parkersburg: "You need not come. Gov. Pierpont has sent us four hundred soldiers from Clarksburg." But at half-past ten, last night, there was a great panic again. It was announced that the rebels were near Marietta, and every one turned out. At every step you met an armed man. Eighty had come from Athens to help us, and they were marshalled with the rest. The night wore away, but the enemy did not come. General result: Nobody killed, nobody wounded, nobody missing, but everybody, almost, severely scared. Finding Mrs. W. uneasy, I slept there. Had a good bed, a good breakfast, and now I am ready for another panic. . . . The rebels are in Indiana. They may be here yet.

If they are not spry, I shall be gone; and what a prize they will lose! It looks now as if Lincoln *must* put his foot down harder. If there must be war, I believe in having it as infernal as possible, so that the world will never want another.

Yours, as always,

T. J. MUMFORD.

A few days after these words were written he left Marietta, where he had passed nearly two pleasant years. He wrote, "There is a great deal that is depressing to me in this leaving a parish. It is hard to part from those who love you." But circumstances made it seem best for him to seek a home in the more bracing climate of New England.

GROTON, Sept. 21, 1862.

Dear Father May, — You ought to be informed of the arrival of all your grandchildren. Yesterday there came to us a child whose naming did not take much time, for we were ready for either sex. A boy was to be Edgar Huidekoper; a girl was to be May, in memory of somebody at Syracuse. It was a boy! Still I feel like telling you of our good intentions, even if they were contingent ones, and not to prove even a *nominal* expression of gratitude and love.

If Mr. Moors, of Greenfield, goes to the war, I am to take his pulpit for nine months. If he does *not* go, I am to take care of Deerfield, James Hosmer having enlisted as a private.

GREENFIELD, March 2, 1863.

Walter Scott tells us that, when Ivanhoe rode into the lists at the famous tournament, "the device on his shield was a young oak-tree pulled up by the roots, with the Spanish word *Desdichado*, signifying Disin-herited"; and I write to ask if it can be true that you intend to doom me to appear in similar guise when I go forth to my future encounters with the world, the flesh, and the devil? It is about five months since I told you that while we were expecting our child, guessing that it would prove a girl, we had decided to name her May Mumford, — when behold it was a boy, and had to be called Edgar Huidekoper! This, with other things supposed to be dipped in honey, and not flavored in the least with the most diluted gall, was duly mailed, and I suppose it reached the saline city. Probably you have been too busy, or too anxious, or too sad to reply; but please to be reminded that there is a blessed urchin nearly six months old who is still ignorant whether or not you have found it in your heart to forgive his masculine gender. He is so bright and merry that sometimes he charms us into transient forgetfulness that there is any war in the land.

I am not a bit disheartened about the war. My chief wonder is that we have not done worse. It would not shake my faith in the result if the most shameful compromise should be made. Even if Jef-ferson Davis should be the next President of a recon-structed Union, it might be the best way to prevent our wounds from being lightly healed.

> "Oh, blessed is he to whom is given
> The instinct that can tell
> That God is on the field, when he
> Is most invisible!"

Greenfield is a very pleasant place to preach in. The congregations are large, and the music is capital.

CONCORD, N. H., Nov. 30, 1863.

While I wait for a train to take me home from this pleasant town where Parker Pillsbury atones for Frank Pierce, I will borrow a pen, and wield it as briskly as possible.

The cause of the country is getting stronger every day. What changes for the better you have witnessed in your lifetime! How clear and strong must be your testimony in favor of the expediency of principle and the power of the truth!

I have opportunities to go to Northampton and another place. It is not decided yet whether I shall have a call to the Dorchester parish or not. I hope to preach at Yonkers before I settle down. . . . I have not seen the "Life of Parker," but a friend who has seen it keeps tantalizing me with crumbs from the tempting feast.

YONKERS, Sunday Evening, Jan. 3, 1864.

My dear L., — There is half an hour before the vesper service, and I must give it to you.

On my way from Meadville I came near making that $4,000 out of the life-insurance offices. Coming down hill at the rate of thirty miles an hour, three cars got off the track, and two of them were badly smashed, bruising some of the passengers. Our car was less injured; but we were off the track for nearly a mile, and we stopped on an embankment near a bridge over a small stream. I never had such a jolting before, but I confess that I was so wicked as to be amused at seeing the stove dance itself to pieces; and you would have been shocked to see that, in picking up my baggage, I went back to get the lunch that F.'s dear hands had prepared for me.

I am at Mr. E. C.'s palace. It is on a hillside, and you can look up and down the noble Hudson for miles. The Palisades are right across the river. It seems almost wrong to be here without you. The church is the most exquisite little affair that I ever saw or dreamed of. Music perfectly "divine," as good as the best in the New York churches. To-night I am to extemporize.

Tuesday, 10 A.M.

I am invited to spend the week here. You would like the C.'s. Mr. C. is president of the village and of a bank, is at the head of a large forwarding house in New York City, and the controlling spirit of a factory here, which employs six hundred and fifty men. With all his cares, he is genial and even seems to have leisure for his family. He is a fearless fellow, likes Wendell Phillips, takes the *Liberator*, and is about to close the two hundred liquor shops of the place, — on Sunday, at least. At the time of the New York riots, the mob threatened to come here and burn this splendid house over his head, but he was too well prepared to defend it. His wife shares his spirit. She says all false conformities and weak silences in the presence of folly and sin are to be abhorred and despised. L. W.

would clap her hands and say grace over both of them.

I am a good deal perplexed about the parishes.* Dorchester is not the most attractive place on many accounts, but I really feel called of God to undertake a work there. If I thought that we could live on the salary offered, I should feel like saying "Yes" at once; not because I might not get a more prominent place, but because I feel sure I can be most permanently useful there.

Do make your plans to meet me in Worcester, and come prepared to go to Boston and Dorchester, that we may "look around." I am still inclined to go there. Staples, of Brooklyn, is breaking down utterly in health, just when his success is complete in the pulpit. I must live more slowly, and last longer, if I care for you and the boy Edgar; and I reckon I do a trifle.

I am writing in Mr. C.'s beautiful library, where I can look down the Hudson for at least ten miles. After a long and severe storm it is clearing away, and the sunlight relieves the severity of the frowning Palisades. Still I am a little sad, because I hoped to be at home to-day. A thousand kisses for the baby.

GROTON, Feb. 13, 1864.

Dear Father May, — Your cordial letter followed me to Brooklyn, where I was staying with a family of true-hearted Germans, whose friendship will be one of my immortal joys.

---

* He was invited to take charge of the pulpit in Yonkers, Concord, N.H., and Northampton about the same time that he was called to Dorchester.

You were right in supposing that it was my mother's departure which you saw announced in the papers. She was very ill only a week or ten days. I was with her the last forty-eight hours of her earthly life, and my coming seemed to be all that she waited for. If you have read the paper on "The Episcopal Church" in the last *Unitarian Monthly*, you may have noticed how I was impressed at her funeral.

The death of Staples is a great loss to us. His going away reminds me of the duty of asking you, in view of life's uncertainties, if you have ever commenced in earnest those autobiographical letters which I have so often urged you to begin to write to somebody. By preparing one a month with scrupulous regularity, and sending it where it will be carefully preserved, you will make a needed preparation for the influence which should live after you are called away. I am not so selfish as to ask that these letters should be addressed to me. Write them to any of your tried and true ones, and I shall be contented.

Parker's life was largely in his correspondence; but there are many of the best incidents of your career of which your letters contain nothing.

I am to be installed over the Dorchester parish on the 2d day of March. If the time had not been so short, the distance so great, and the season so inclement, I should have tried to have you come on and take some part; but these considerations pre-

vented my attempting it.   J. F. Clarke is to preach
the sermon, and Brother Tilden is to represent you in
an address to the people.

Our boy is a superb fellow, and he sits in the sunshine singing as I write.   He has dark hazel eyes, a
voice of ravishing sweetness, and a " smile that cheers
like dawn of day."

VIII.

THE EPISCOPAL CHURCH.*

There are hours in every man's life when he feels, with peculiar depth and liveliness of emotion, the power of the past. At such a season, I have been drawn, quite recently, in that direction in which so many persons are nowadays attracted,— I mean towards the Episcopal Church.

My first and best friend had ended her long earthly life of most affectionate self-renunciation, and her freed spirit had gone to God who gave it. Although she had no theology that might not be summed up in half a verse of one of John's epistles, — "God is love; and he that dwelleth in love dwelleth in God, and God in him," — it was fitting that her body should be buried according to the rites of the church of which she had been for many years a member. We carried the precious dust to a beautiful edifice, where a clergyman whom she had honored and loved, not so much for his doctrinal accuracy as for his generous fidelity to the poor, read the service so eminently appropriate for those who go to their fathers in peace and are buried in a good old age,— adding some words of his own that were freighted with all

---

*Part of the paper with this caption, to which allusion is made in the preceding letter.

the tenderness and beauty of the Christian faith.
As I sat there in that stately house of prayer, listening to expressions that awakened memories of
other departures, and softened by the plaintive, yet
far from hopeless strains of a noble organ, I confess
that it was with a feeling somewhat akin to the
longings of homesickness. My eyes rested on the
tablets behind the altar, which resembled those
from which I learned my earliest scriptural lessons
when a child at church. The reading-desk reminded
me of my father's pale and earnest face, when, as
one of the wardens, he used to read the services in
the absence or illness of the minister. As we bowed
our heads in prayer, I could almost fancy that he
was again beside me at the head of the pew; and
I caught myself listening for his low, yet clear
responses. The intervening years of my heretical
ministry were all forgotten; and, for the hour, I felt
that my truant feet were once more treading within
the sacred precincts of the homestead for my soul.
Thus it continued as long as mere emotion reigned;
and I could hear in my sadness only the sweet voices
of the past, which seemed to bid me return. As
soon, however, as reason and conscience reasserted
that there are principles as well as sentiments, I saw
how impassable is the chasm which separates me
from the church of my youth.

No bishopric, even in an Empire State, not all the
treasures of Trinity Church, could tempt me from
the place where I sit, at the feet of John G. Whittier,
as he writes these golden lines: "I cannot be suffi-

ciently thankful to the Divine Providence which
turned me so early away from what Roger Williams
calls 'the world's great trinity, pleasure, profit, and
honor,' to take side with the poor and oppressed.   I
set a higher value on my name as appended to the
anti-slavery declaration of 1833 than on the title-
page of any book.   Looking over a life marked by
many errors and shortcomings, I rejoice that I have
been able to maintain the pledge of that signature;
and that, in the long intervening years, —

> "'My voice, though not the loudest, has been heard
> Wherever Freedom raised her cry of pain.'"

IX

LIFE IN DORCHESTER.

Pastoral and Friendly Letters.— Interest in his Parish.— Gratitude to Channing.—Anecdote of Robert Collyer.— Confidence in the Truth.—Help to a Needy Soul.—Literary Work.—Helps the Monthly Journal and Sunday School Gazette.—Proposes the Theological Club.—Assistant Editor of The Christian Register.—The May Memorial.

For glimpses into the closing years of his ministerial life, extending from March 2, 1864, to March 2, 1872, we clip not only from the remaining letters to Samuel J. May, but also from those addressed to some of his parishioners, and others who were his intimate personal friends : —

DORCHESTER, April 28, 1864.

My dear Mrs. W.,—You need not fear that I shall be running off from my parish very soon. So long as I can interest the people, I shall not *seek* any other field. It seems to me there is something to be done here. If I can gather some of these young men and women into the fold of the Good Shepherd, I shall be a far happier man; not so much because of any visible success on my part as on account of the strength and peace and joy secured for them. It is so devoutly to be desired that they may understand that an earnest life is not necessarily a dull one, but that the better we are, the more truly genial shall we become !

GROTON, MASS., Aug. 19, 1864.

We are all sorry to leave Groton, but very glad to look forward to our new home. If I cannot be useful there, I shall be very much disappointed. I hope they will not persist in putting me on the school committee, however; for, although I mean to visit the schools frequently, I prefer to do so in an unofficial capacity. Indeed, I know of several friends who have had serious trouble in their parishes on account of committee affairs. Few parents are reasonable when a child's interest and reputation are at stake; and a faithful ministry has enough trials and collisions of its own, particularly in a village. . . .

Master Edgar seems to be in fine health. Yesterday he spent an hour at the railroad station, where he manifested the liveliest appreciation of the beauty of the locomotive. I do not think he will see anything so lovely again until he gets a fortunate glimpse of Mr. C.'s mule.

Oct. 27, 1864.

Dear Father May,—At the eleventh hour, I send you by express, charges prepaid, two hundred and fifty excellent campaign documents, for circulation in Onondaga County. Do see that they are given to men who will take pains to use them wisely and well.

Last Sunday I preached at King's Chapel, dining with the senior warden,—your friend Mr. George B. Emerson. We had some sweet talk of you, and your ears ought to have been burned to cinders. He is a noble man, and I thank him for valuable hints concerning my delivery.

DORCHESTER, Jan. 3, 1867.

My dear Miss C.,— It is a vast comfort and encouragement to be assured that I have done anybody the least good. But what Shakspeare says of jests is equally true of sermons,— that their prosperity depends more on the ears that hear than on the tongues that speak. . . . It is always pleasant to see you at church. It encourages me to have you say that any service of mine interests and helps you, for my ministerial misgivings have always been numerous, and often painful. My humblest hours have been spent in the pulpit. . . .

You need not fear that I shall leave my parish for a larger one if I can get it. My ambition is satisfied. Samuel J. May defines success in life as "loving and being loved," and I accept the definition. When I am sounded about being satisfied with my position, I always answer, "Yes"; and that ends it. Still, I dwell in a tent, and if the Lord tells me, to-morrow, to go to Oregon, I trust I shall have grace given me to start. . . .

The name of Channing is very sacred to me. Sometimes it has seemed next in sanctity and blessing to the name of Christ. Certainly no human teacher has done more for my mind and heart than your uncle. I seldom read his works now; but it is on account of the intense delight with which my soul almost lived upon them when I was breaking the shackles of my pro-slavery and Episcopal education. I scarcely need the books to remind me of what he said and did for his race.

MILTON, MASS., June 4, 1867.

Dear X., — I dare not look at the date of your good letter, which made me very happy when it came; but my chief consolation is, that it told of the arrival of wife and child, and so I know you have been independent of communication from foreigners. I have thought of you ever so many thousand times. Whenever a grand word is said at any of our gatherings, I catch myself thinking, "I wish X. could hear that." Last week, at the Music Hall, one Judge N., who evidently belongs to the itinerant laity, and now from Knoxville, Tenn., told us in a very simple and touching way how Samuel J. May converted him, and that he (the judge) was instrumental in converting you, somewhere near St. Paul, and how last year he made way for you to preach somewhere on the Pacific coast. Did your ears burn when we applauded his recruit?

The Anniversary meetings have really been good, this year. They were heralded by preaching to crowds in the Boston Theatre, where Robert Collyer got his share of the glory. I followed him to Lynn, etc., just to listen to his voice, and to look upon his manly face, — for, after all, the charm is in the man. I am reading his volume, "Nature and Life"; but I should not half-enjoy it, if I could not interpolate the tones and smiles, and now and then the tears, too.

The morning after he preached for the first time in the theatre, I was with C. and T. We heard that

Collyer was quartered at the Tremont House (he was at Bartol's), so we went to call on him.

Inquiring Minister. — Is Mr. Collyer here?

Clerk. — Yes.

I. M. — Can we see him?

C. — Yes, by going to the Howard. He is there rehearsing.

I. M. — It cannot be. It is the Rev. Mr. Collyer, of Chicago, that we are after.

C. — Oh, you mean the gentleman who appeared at the *Boston*, last night! He has not been here.

Thus we learned that there is an actor named Collyer. This story is true, and I hope it is not bad.

Robert told me that an ex-Christian, now agent of the American Unitarian Association, at a meeting in Indiana, told the folks that he had all sorts of Unitarian tracts, some of which he could indorse heartily, but others he could not. A fine old Quaker came forward and asked Brother E. to put aside the tracts which he did *not* like, and then said, " Thank thee. I think I will take *these*." . . .

We had Music Hall crammed for three days in succession. The prettiest sight of all was the three thousand children, Wednesday afternoon.

. . . There are a few bigoted conservatives and a few mischievous radicals who are determined to be persecuted; but the great mass of our people mean to be broad and fair and free. If any votes at all are taken, somebody is liable to be in the majority, and somebody in the minority; but the truth will triumph in the end, if its advocates are patient and believing.

June 26, 1868.

My dear Mrs. S.,— Your welcome flowers and still more precious note were a delight, but not a surprise to me, this morning; for you have already taught me to depend upon the constancy of your friendship and its timely and thoughtful expressions. I respond most heartily to all your cordial good-will. It is very gratifying to know that I am associated in your mind with one so near and dear as your eldest son.

Some of my friends are a little impatient with me for refusing to "candidate" in several larger parishes, where I am supposed to have a "chance"; but the truth is, I am thoroughly satisfied where I am. The society is not altogether what I would like to see it, but it is better than I deserve; and I am sure that the whole world cannot give me warmer or truer friends than many to whom I now minister. While they are spared to bless me. with their love, the thought of going away is too painful to be entertained.

Aug. 27, 1868.

You have shown an almost startling knowledge of my wants in sending me a neck-tie of your own making. It was precisely my most immediate and pressing need; for my little "bow," like some really interesting visitors, often refuses to "stay on."

Oct. 12, 1868.

My dear Mrs. ——, Most heartily do I thank you for every assurance that I am able to help you in any way. I am truly sorry that you sometimes lack courage, and perhaps feel overawed, even when you are drawn nearest to the Lord by your longings and your needs. For my own part, I am grateful for the confidence in his welcome which I share with the publicans and the sinners of old; and the sight of his love attracts me so powerfully that the weight of sin and the hindrances of unworthiness are overcome at once. I cannot wrong Jesus by the least distrust. I know it is his supreme delight to lift us up, and to lead us home. I am conscious of his response to every imploring word and every appealing look. Indeed, he is most near when most needed; and there is no barrier so fatal as self-complacency or self-righteousness. If we would not grieve him, we should feel boldest when humblest, and most abounding in his love when most in need of it. He was "lifted up" that we might look above ourselves, and away from ourselves, and remember only the inviting voice and the open arms. . . .

You wish to do more than you have bodily strength to accomplish; but remember that God can accomplish his own purposes; and, if you do all you can, he will count it enough. We cannot earn our full salvation. We must be willing to be "forgiven much," and to be forgiven freely. You do not ask your children to repay everything. It is the chief bliss of the relation, that some "obligations" are to be forever uncancelled,— that, indeed, they are not obligations at all, but gifts of generous love.

Do not fear that I shall deem you so much better than you really are. I have no doubt that you are

human,—that you have sometimes cried, and have
had reason to cry, "God be merciful to me a sinner!"
I, too, have a reciprocal fear that you may mistake
my aspirations for my attainments.　Any confidence
that is ever granted me comes, not from self-con-
templation, but from the temporary absence of it.
I am as utterly sick of myself as you can possibly
be; but I do believe there is not only pardon, but
peace for the penitent, and that God is never so
happy as when he beholds our homeward faces "a
great way off," and runs to meet us.　I should feel
so, and I should ask you to feel so, whatever sins we
might have committed, and however far and long we
might have wandered.　If we are only truly sorry,
and really wish to do better, unless the gospel is
all a delusion and Jesus the worst of deceivers, the
past should be forgotten; for it is forgiven.　Perhaps this will not tell you anything you do not
know better than I do by far; but I think Jesus
encouraged us to grant absolution upon his conditions, so strangely generous, so almost incredibly
merciful.　I beg you to approach him boldly; not
to fear to have him know everything, not to doubt
that he loves you as truly as he ever loved, and
still loves, Mary and Martha and Lazarus, and all
the rest who saw his face and heard his tones.

Nov. 24, 1868.

My dear Mrs. W.,—My health has not been so
good for many years.　I find I can take good care
of my parish, and have some strength left for outside

work, including some assistance given to Brother Bush, every week, at the *Register* office. I make up the "Spirit of the Press," and write the short editorial paragraphs.

March 12, 1869.

I hope you are right in your estimate of my preaching. Once in a great while I feel half-persuaded that it is so myself. But few can imagine with what a sense of unfitness for the pulpit I have had to struggle, for nearly eighteen years. It is not always so, of course. Some Sundays I feel sure that I have the right word, and that I shall be helped to utter it; but, at other times, a very stubborn doubt thrusts itself in my way. Still, past deliverances ought to make me hopeful of future ones.

Certainly I cannot complain of a want of appreciation, far beyond my deserts, outside of my parish as well as in it.

CATSKILL MOUNTAIN HOUSE, Sept. 13, 1869.

Dear Edgar, — I hope I shall get a letter from your mamma to-night, and that it will tell me you are all well. I am quite well myself. I eat two chickens every day, and when I get home I may *crow* instead of speaking to you.

GRANT HOUSE, Sept. 19.

To-morrow is your birthday,* and I am sorry I cannot spend it with you. This is my last Sunday away from home; and I shall be all ready to return when the time comes, for I want to see you all very much.

*Aged six years.

After keeping cool upon the mountain, it seems very hot down here. This morning I walked to the village, and went to church. The walk back was warm and dusty, but the mountains were right before me, and they were so beautiful that I forgot everything else.

I suppose you will have a great deal to tell me about the storm when I get home. I hope you are going to school. I went as soon as I was five years old, and had to be taken on horseback in front of a colored man named Romeo, who was my father's slave. Give kisses to mamma and grandma.

Your loving father.

April 6, 1870.

Dear Father May,— If I had charge of the *Register*, I should print your excellent note, so far as relates to the threatened division. It is my hope and belief that not more than a tenth of us will go off into Free Religion, and not more than another tenth into Evangelicalism, if our leaders are wise and broad like James F. Clarke.

After visiting his favorite spot in the Milton Cemetery, where "under the pines" his body now rests, he wrote to his friend Mrs. W.,—

Sept. 28, 1870.

The sacred place was reached while there was plenty of light to see the decorations. I could have found the spot in the dark, guided by the fragrance of the flowers. I think that next to the thought that M.'s body lies there, I like that vicinity because you seem to pass through the dark valley to the light and warmth of the hill beyond.

At the date of Mr. Mumford's settlement in Dorchester, the war had not ended. Instant in season and out of season, his humble word was spoken for the soldier and the cause he represented. He encouraged the hands of faithful women who were busy feeding and clothing the sick and wounded; and when Abraham Lincoln, in the single-sightedness of his vision of truth and right, spoke the immortal words which broke the shackles of the slave, he gave of his zeal and his resources to the cause of freedom and the education of the people so long bound in helpless ignorance. The warmth and breadth of his sympathies made him the friend of that grand army of soldiers who came home from the battle-field to live once more with kindred in renewed bonds of love, and that other army who in the spirit of heroic sacrifice had marched to the undiscovered country.

Occasionally short articles and letters of his appeared in the *Inquirer* and *Register.* About this time he also prepared a series of articles for the *Monthly Journal,* which the Assistant Secretary of the American Unitarian Association was eager to convert into a literary as well as a news journal. With James Freeman Clarke, and a few others, he helped to brighten its sunset glow, and prove to the denomination that such a journal could be made a welcome magazine of valuable reading matter, as well as of statistics. Here appeared "Stray Hints to Parishes," "Sunday-Schools Again," "What shall we do with our Second Service?" "The Minister we do not Want," "Fruit in Old Age," "The Southern Need of Dr. Noyes," "The Episcopal Church," and the serial called "The Journal of a Candidate," which he was often urged to publish as a book.

The brilliancy and wit of his pen attracted some notice. He afterwards wrote "Funereal Follies," for *Old and New.*

In the latter part of the year 1865, the Sunday School Society had become almost a forlorn hope, and the little *Gazette* was at death's door. He was urged, if possible, to breathe into both the breath of life. By first setting the example of generosity and devotion, and then calling upon others to help him, he put the Society once more on its financial feet. Receiving as a minister a salary inadequate to the support of his family, he could not give a bank check for a thousand dollars. Its equivalent he gave in his services for one year, making the *Gazette* what it had never been before, and leaving in the treasury a larger balance with which to begin the next year's work. But, above all, he restored the Society to the confidence of the people, and awakened a wider interest in it.

His relations with churches of differing faiths about him were warm and fraternal. No deeper mark of affection and respect could have been paid to him than was given when he was asked to offer the consecrating prayer at the laying of the corner-stone of the new Methodist church in his neighborhood. As an additional mark of respect, a copy of the paper he edited was placed beneath the stone. With bishops and elders he stood as a recognized brother in Christ. It was one of the joys of his heart that he was so beloved.

The interest which he took in the young preachers. who came to him by the eternal law in which sympathy begets sympathy, led him to the measures which resulted in the formation of the Theological Club,— an institution which still exists, and which has been valuable for exactly the purposes for which he suggested it.

He felt that the young ministers of the Unitarian Church had no simple way of meeting familiarly with their older brethren, and that there was also, in many instances, none of that stimulus for theological study which is given when men meet easily together, to compare their views and their studies. Where there happened to be a ministerial association which kept up any theological work, this last difficulty was met; but a good many of the younger men belonged to no such association, and he was afraid that some of them felt "left out in the cold." This led him to propose a club, to be open to the older and the younger men alike, with the simple purpose of conversation on theological subjects of interest,— with the understanding that it should always elect young ministers, if it could be made out that they wanted to study.

The proposal was cordially met by several of the settled ministers in and near Boston to whom he submitted it. From it the "Theological Club" grew; and all the members of that Club are grateful to him as its founder. It is specially interesting that he should have undertaken its formation, for he, of all men in our ministry, did not need it. He was never in want of sympathetic professional associations; but he saw the need for others, and this was enough to start him on the plan.

There is something pleasing in his own modesty about his membership of this Club, when he was notified of its first meeting. He writes:—

MILTON, Dec. 29, 1868.

Dear Hale,— I hope you will think favorably of my suggestion about giving the young ministers of this region a chance to meet you and each other in a social way. . . . I think there might be a very good time. I do not propose anything formal or frequent, nor do I think you should burden yourself with any thought of material "refreshments." I only know that these men have few opportunities to meet each other in private, and all of them will be grateful for the slightest manifestation of your interest and sympathy. There are very few of the Boston ministers who seem to know anything or to care anything about their younger brethren. I am not sure that my plan would result in anything at all satisfactory, but the men would appreciate such an invitation, even if they could not conveniently come.

Yours most cordially,

T. J. MUMFORD.

P. S.— I was quite disinterested in proposing what I thought would be a good thing for our younger men. It did not occur to me that I was to be counted in; but I will go to Mr. Clarke's, as you kindly suggest.

The fiftieth anniversary of the publication of the *Christian Register* was held April 20, 1871. Mr. Mumford had been for nearly three years the assistant editor. At the dinner given to the friends of the paper, Mr. Haskell, the editor of the *Transcript*, paid a marked compliment to his ability, in the following words: "I should not do justice to my own feelings on this occasion were I to keep *mum* in regard to our Friend Mumford, of the *Register*. He has introduced a feature which the best and most prosperous papers are copying all over the country. I never read one of those columns of 'Brevities' that I do not think of what the California miner said of our dear friend, Starr King. He came down from the mines, and went to the crowded church, stood up in the entry and heard the sermon, not knowing who the preacher was, and as he turned he said, 'That man takes a trick every time.' So our Friend Mumford makes a point every time. I think that column combines the most popular element and the best taste; and the man who writes those paragraphs,— his inkstand is worth a mine of gold to any organization."

Rev. Nathaniel Hall, of Dorchester, the loved and revered friend of Mr. Mumford, once wrote to him: "You are a fortunate man to hold such a pen, with such a mind and heart behind it."

We copy the following letter, written by one who, like Mr. Haskell and Mr. Hall, has passed on to life in a higher sphere:

ROOMS OF THE AMERICAN UNITARIAN ASSOCIATION,
42 Chauncy Street, April 17, 1871.

My dear Mr. Mumford,— I know that you dislike compliments, and perhaps to your face I should not venture to say what, even now, I shall put as moderately as I can.

But the occasion of the anniversary of the *Register* makes it appropriate that we should think about the paper, and, if we have any feeling about it, that we should give it expression.

And, as I have been recalling the course and management of the *Register* the last year or two, I recognize so gratefully what you have done that I cannot help writing to thank you for it with all my heart. I have a double reason: first, because of your brave and strong and effective advocacy of the right cause; and second, because of your more than kind words and action in reference to me. I have never said anything about this, because I never knew exactly how to; but you may be sure I have felt it, and remember it with gratitude.

I do often wish that your articles were in larger type, especially such admirable ones as that in yesterday's paper about Mr. Burleigh and the New York Conference, and others just as good in every week's issue; but we are all learning to get used to the type, and think only of the value of the thought.

And now, hoping that your modesty will forgive what is, after all, only the merest hint of what I feel,

I am ever truly yours,

CHARLES LOWE.

May 1, 1871.

Dear Father May,— Do go on with your autobiography. If Joseph and I outlive you, we will see that nothing indiscreet is published; and therefore you can write as freely as you please for your children and grandchildren. Remember that if you do not go on with this autobiography you will grieve me very much, and disappoint a great many whom you would be glad to gratify.

Always yours fondly,

T. J. MUMFORD.

Two months from the date of this last letter, Samuel J. May was called to his heavenly home. The autobiography was left unfinished. It became the sad pleasure of his family and his nearest friends to gather up the memorials of his life, and commit their arrangement to him who was always his "dear, dutiful" or his "beloved son" in the kinship of spirit, as Timothy was the spiritual son of Paul. The work of planning and collecting was assigned to Mr. George B. Emerson, Mr. Samuel May, and Thomas J. Mumford. To the latter, by vote of the older members of the committee, was intrusted the pleasing task of editing the memoir. Actual work upon it began in the fall of 1871. It was ready for the press one year from this time.

June 27, 1871.

My dear Mrs. W.,— I received the "North Wind" on Saturday, and the south wind yesterday. For both I thank you. Your good wishes are balmy and genial indeed, and I always breathe freely and deeply when such "spicy gales" are blowing. They are so exhilarating that I feel that I must do my very best in and for the world, if I would be worthy of such friendship.

This last birthday has made me feel as never before that I am no longer the young man that I have insisted upon remaining. My father's hair was entirely white at forty-five, and mine is fast becoming so. I am grateful for what has gone, and for what is coming.

Oct. 26, 1871.

I intend to tell my people that I shall cease to be their pastor on the 2d of March, eight years from the time of my settlement. I am to be sole editor of the *Register* after the 1st of January. The work is very attractive to me, and I feel surer of my *call* to it than I have ever felt about preaching. I *was* called to be a pastor, and I mean to retain something of *this* relation to many of my old flocks, especially to *stray* sheep who have no new brand on them. I have not been able to call on my people as much since I have had the paper to care for, but I had to piece out my salary somehow.

One of Mr. Mumford's favorite texts was, "Owe no man anything." Unwilling to be personally in debt to any one, he was as reluctant to serve a parish whose books were not clear of any such incumbrance. Soon after his settlement he became active in persuading the people to provide a suitable place for the Sunday-school, and for the Young People's Christian Union, which he organized, as well as for the social and charitable meetings of the society. But, discovering a debt of nearly a thousand dollars, he said, "Let us suspend the raising of money for better accommodations until the debt is cancelled." In answer to his request, the amount was raised on the spot, and the adjourned meeting left the parish free of debt. The contribution of money for a parish hall went on at intervals during his ministry. At the time of his resignation, the requisite amount had been raised and a plan of building adopted.

On the walls of this hall the grateful people have hung the life-size crayon * of their beloved pastor.

* See frontispiece.

X.

EDITORIAL LIFE.

Letters of Welcome. — Completion of the May Memorial. — Its Reception. — Mr. Mumford's Relation to the Free Religionists. — His Catholicity of Spirit. — Death of his Sister. — Last Letters to his Son.

The year 1872 opened with bright prospects. While the heart of the minister turned back with fond memories to the flock he had watched over for eight years, he was looking forward to the satisfactions which the editorial life had ever offered him, and to the carrying out of the long-cherished wish of his heart, the preparation of the Life of his dear friend, Samuel J. May. So the year found him busy, as well as full of hope.

The invitation to become editor of *The Christian Register* was received October 25, 1871. His duties were to begin with the new year. The 1st of December his letter of resignation was read to his parish by his friend and neighbor, Rev. Francis T. Washburn. The announcement fell like a thunderbolt on the ears of his people. He had not told them of his intentions, — not even those who were in many respects his intimate friends, — because he thought that in his relations to them as pastor all his people had equal claims upon his confidence. According to the conditions of settlement he was to give three months' notice to his parish of any intention to dissolve his official relations with them; so he remained their pastor till March, taking entire charge of the paper, and continuing work upon the May Memoir.

The perfect satisfaction that he found in his editorial work, in spite of its heavy responsibilities and its many trying and harassing cares, may be known from his own testimony: "I have lived to be forty-five years old without ever finding out what I was made for till now." This satisfaction was quite as evident to his friends and readers as to himself. It revealed itself in his work, which was seen to be that of a lover, not that of a drudge. His position as assistant editor had already given the readers of the *Register* a taste of his quality, and the satisfaction with which his appointment as editor-in-chief was received may be learned from the following extracts from a few of the many letters he received : —

BOSTON, Dec. 13, 1871.

Dear Mumford,— I am glad of your being editor of the *Register*, and applaud your resignation of your parish to devote yourself to a more important task.

I delight in the prospect which your intellectual, moral, spiritual, and Christian qualifications for this particular function open.

Beware of the universal temptations to hyper-criticism, combativeness, conceit, smartness, and sardonic contempt of personal or doctrinal foes, and of the proud irresponsibleness of a public pen ; and believe you have a friend and well-wisher and large hoper for you in   Yours,   C. A. BARTOL.

P. S. — Don't (eschewing vitriol) leave out the *spice.*   C. A. B.

SAN JOSE, CAL., Jan. 12, 1871.

Dear Man and Brother,— I do think there are few brighter papers in the land than the *Register ;* and 'tis the only paper which I much miss, if it doesn't come when it ought. *You* I don't miss, feeling that I have you in happy earnest.

Salute the household, and may your hearts all be full of quiet songs !   Serenely,   C. G. AMES.

OFFICE OF THE INDEX, TOLEDO, OHIO, April 20, 1872.

My dear Mr. Mumford,— Although it is late Saturday night, I must send a hurried line to thank you for the noble and generous spirit of your late articles.

I want just to take your hand for a hearty shake, because I fear you were wounded by my silence regarding the beautiful letter you sent me a few months ago. I felt it deeply, however, and feel troubled because I have left it so long unanswered.

While we must still "exchange shots," etc., for our causes, let us ever be the sincere friends we are to-day. "Squib" away — I shall, too; but no malice shall poison the arrow's point.

Yours unreservedly,

FRANCIS E. ABBOT.

The following letter is from Mr. Mumford to his friend Mrs. S.:—

Oct. 20, 1872.

My editorial duties require nearly all my time; and of late all available leisure has been needed for the May Memoir. This is now nearly done, and I hope that nothing but the proof-reading will remain.

If it were not for a fresh cold, I should come over, this evening, to tell you about our interview with George MacDonald. Mrs. W. looked unusually well and happy, and of course she made her little party a most delightful one.

Dec. 24, 1872.

My dear Mrs. W.,— My book has gone to the press, after costing me more wear and tear of feeling on account of the sensibilities of others than actual work. By and by, I hope you will glance at the story of my Father May's life.

The publication of the May Memoir brought forth, among others, the letters from which we make the following extracts : —

April 30, 1873.

Rev. Mr. Mumford :

My dear Sir,— I have your highly esteemed note of the 25th instant. I did not before know that you were born in South Carolina, and were the son of a slave-holder. You certainly had a poor start in abolitionism. "All's well that ends well." You have come out right, and it gives me pleasure to know that one of my anti-slavery speeches is entitled to a little of the credit of it.

I hope your life of our dear May sells well. The charm of your book is, that it allows its dear subject to speak for himself, and does not bury him in the words of its author.

I am an old man (seventy-six), but I should be right glad to receive a visit from you, should you ever be journeying this way. I hope I may yet have the pleasure of taking you by the hand. I value you all the more, because you were the friend of my dear May.

Cordially yours, Gerrit Smith.

Bridport, Eng., Aug. 1, 1873.

Dear Sir, — I have been reading the memoir of S. J. May with deep interest. Of all the anti-slavery advocates, he was the one with whose spirit I felt the greatest sympathy ; and I feel like

Mr. Whittier, who said that every one loved him at first sight.

I have reviewed your Memoir in the *Inquirer*, where it will appear, I suppose, to-morrow. I have also sent an article to the *Herald*. Last Sunday week, I made him the subject of a biographical discourse from the pulpit.

You will not be surprised, therefore, that I wish the book to be more widely diffused in this country. Is the book stereotyped? If so, might it not be well to send over five hundred copies to England, in sheets, at a lower price than it could be reprinted for here? I know no book better worth reprinting.

Mr. May, perhaps, did as much good as Dr. Channing; but his works were those which chiefly influenced his own countrymen, who were the eye-witnesses of his ministry. Believe me,

Yours faithfully,   R. L. CARPENTER.

TRIBUNE OFFICE, NEW YORK, Dec. 11, 1871.

My dear Friend,— I am glad that the work of writing the life of our beloved friend has fallen, in part, to your hands; for I know how deep was your reverence for him, and how well you are qualified to tell what you know.

I, too, remember the days when we first met under the roof of Thomas and Mary Anne M'Clintock, at Waterloo. The interest in you, awakened then, has continued without abatement to this day, and I have rejoiced in view of your work and your success therein.   Yours truly,   OLIVER JOHNSON.

A few years later, the same warm friend wrote Mr. Mumford the following frank and generous lines in regard to his conduct of the *Register:* —

OFFICE CHRISTIAN UNION, NEW YORK, Feb. 24, 1874.

Dear old Friend,— I owe you thanks for your kind allusion in the *Register* to my "Anti-Slavery Reminiscences," and to myself personally. You make the *Register* a very bright paper, and I congratulate you most heartily upon your success. I do not always relish your sarcasm, and I sometimes think you are not quite fair in your jibes at the Free Religionists; but it would be very foolish in you to try to please *me* in all things. To make a good paper, you must be independent.

Yours affectionately,

OLIVER JOHNSON.

Perhaps the best commentary on these candid and good-natured criticisms may be found in the two letters of Mr. Mumford which follow. Though not addressed to Mr. Johnson, they were written to a brother minister, also a member of the Free Religious Association, for whom, as will be seen, he entertained a strong and abiding friendship. They show that, if his pen sometimes erred, his heart was not at fault. His convictions were strong, but his sympathies were warm and broad; and no one was more prompt to admit an error of his own, or to recognize and applaud the merit of an antagonist.

Dec. 26, 1871.

Dear X.,— You *are* good. If they ever intrust the making up of the list of saints to me, — I am dreadfully afraid they won't. — your name shall go in sure. . . . The address is rather longer than I expected, and on this account I shall have to defer it until my second number; but it shall have the place of honor in that, and not one jot or tittle shall be omitted. I have just read it with almost too much emotion for a public place, jumping up now and then, and insisting that Sister W., who keeps the *Register's* books, shall hear a few good rings of the notes of life that are in it. It is my creed, my statement of faith. . . . Y. is bitter. He writes to blame me frankly for my sharpness in dealing with the Free Religionists. They evidently think it is more blessed to give than to receive — criticism! And I may tell them so. My ill-nature and poisoned arrows are all gammon. I love all these fellows a great deal more than I do some of the fossils whom I have criticised just as freely. . . .

Yours very fondly,

T. J. MUMFORD.

BOSTON, April 11, 1874.

Dear X.,— . . . I shall be heartily glad if you will write an article from your old text, "Sirs, ye are brethren," and show, as frequently as you please, that, at the bottoms of their hearts, Orthodox, Unitarians, and Free Religionists are at peace instead of at war. . . . Of course I have no prejudice against freedom or religion in the abstract; but when the imperfect *Register* gets to dealing with the imperfect *Index*, I presume that an impartial judge can see a plenty of partisanship on both sides. I do not mean to be mean and unfair, but I can hardly get out of the prize-fight without striking; and, whether A., F., etc., come up smiling or frowning, they seem to say,

"Don't trouble yourself about any concern for *our* skulls, but look out, or yours will get cracked." Of late I have tried hard to curb my combativeness, and I hope there has been a little less of it. My dear fellow, when you have been stumping for the Republican party as it was, have you always kept wholly free from the rage of battle? Perhaps you did; for you are more of a Quaker than I am, or ever will be, I fear.

I am not so very malignant, however. Having begun as a pro-slavery Episcopalian, I was converted by Quaker women of the most radical type. I am catholic in my friendships, keep my old Episcopal High-Church pastor's picture in my study, and if A. is half as fond of me as I am of him, we cannot quarrel.

You must remember that it is not here as it is in England. There is no anti-Unitarian and anti-Christian organ there. Here there is an able and aggressive-one, and with it has come some inevitable sparring. I have never written a word in an ugly spirit; and I hope that, if any bad blood gets into my veins, some faithful surgeon will bleed me freely and promptly. . . . To my apprehension, the Christian religion, in its simplicity and purity, is free and broad and inclusive. That is the reason I like it, and don't want to have it defamed and abandoned. . . .

With love for your dear self,

T. J. M.

MILTON, Sept. 29, 1873.

Dear Mrs. W., — This month is full of precious anniversaries. It is a little more than three weeks since L. and I visited the Milton "God's Acre," and brought away the leaves which I enclose to you. It was a beautiful afternoon, and the place was so lovely that we felt inclined to linger for hours.

If I am an editor when I go to Mrs. ——'s, I always feel like a minister when I come away; for she knows how to transform me by the renewing of my mind, and my soul too. Well, the ministerial satisfactions are higher and deeper, and I may return to them, once in a while, to re-form my character. So many poor parsons are about that I do not preach unless some friend is sick or absent from his post.

Sunday Noon, July, 1874.

Dear Edgar, — When I got home, last night, the first thing I saw was your old cap left on my study-table. I was very glad indeed to see it, for I love my boy, with all his faults; and whatever reminds me of him is therefore welcome. Still I should not love him any less if he overcame his carelessness, and I should feel easier about his future. He may think that father and mother are sometimes impatient, but he will never find anybody who is really more patient, although some may indulge him more for a time, not caring much whether he becomes a good and useful man or not.

If I was glad to see your cap on the table, I was

rejoiced when I opened the barn-door and saw that you had really done something towards leaving a supply of kindling-wood. That looked thoughtful and kind. To be sure, I may have to add to the pile; for, in your generous desire that I shall not suffer in my health from lack of exercise, you did not leave an excessive supply; but it will be much pleasanter to add than it would have been to find nothing to add to.

I hope you are having a delightful day at the sea-shore, and that you do all you can to make your mother happy. The weather is about right, and if all is peaceful within, you can hardly fail to be happy.

Give your mother a kiss for me, and ask her to give you one on my account.

PHILADELPHIA, May 12, 1875.

Dear Edgar,— Your mother is on her way to you. The "Saxon" started just before eleven o'clock, and we waved our handkerchiefs to each other as long as they could be seen. She has a delightful room, and will receive every attention. I hope she will get to Boston safely. The wind is blowing hard, but it may not be very rough at sea. I hope you are well and good and happy. Your mother said a great many fond things of you before the boat started. God bless you, darling!

MILTON, May 1, 1876.

Dear X.,— I got up early this morning, to read the proof of the first sixty pages of a volume of sermons and essays by F. T. Washburn. They are as clear, bright, pure, and sweet as the morning itself. I should be tempted to think that heaven grieved and earth lost much by his removal, if I did not hope that these printed words will reach and help many human hearts. Of course there will not be much chance to sell such a book, but the quality of the influence will be rich and high. . . .

Ever yours,   T. J. MUMFORD.

BOSTON, April 7, 1877.

Dear X.,— If you knew how much good your letter did me, you would be glad you wrote it, even if it did cost an effort in the lassitude of spring, after the hard work of winter. All my thoughts of you are refreshing and inspiring, and hearing from you is one of my chief pleasures. You are one of the men that I trust absolutely; and I think I should do so even if you sometimes felt bound by your love for me, and the truth and the right, to give me blows that draw blood When you can be encouraging, it helps me to overcome a morbid self-distrust which has dogged me through life, sometimes nearly ruining me. . . . I winced a little, to have it known that good M. G. thought I deserved a public whipping for my sins; but, after all, she has not made me see that what I said of Mr. P. is not substantially true. An old abolitionist is rather better than ordinary men, if he behaves himself; but, if he doesn't, he is amenable to the laws of truth and decency, and there is not much harm in telling him so with some of his own plainness of speech. .... I hope X. and Y. will get over their bad attack of "statement of belief" on the brain. The spiritual leadership of Jesus, and the promotion of pure Christianity, are basis enough for me. Agitation for anything more will be mischievous and abortive. ....   Yours heartily,

T. J. MUMFORD.

Though Mr. Mumford gave up his parish, he never ceased to be a minister. He was born to help and to console. He made haste to serve brother ministers in their need. He was often in the house of mourning, investing the solemn rites of burial with the illuminating faith and hope of the Dayspring from on high. He was unwearied in bearing messages of good cheer, of sympathy, of comfort, and of counsel. Taking little or no rest himself. he was untiring in serving others. Into the last summer of his life were crowded such labors of love. While in the midst of a remonstrance from his friend and co-worker at the office, and a half-uttered promise to refuse all solicitations to conduct funeral services in the absence of pastors, he was called upon to go to a distant city for this purpose. Turning to his friend, he said, "You must let me go this time. This is a particular service which I cannot refuse. I promise to do better in future." It was his last service of love for the living in memory of the dead. One week later the floral cross lay upon his own casket.

In addition to the letters already introduced from Mr. Mumford to his dear friend, Mrs. A. D. T. Whitney, we copy from one or two written to her during the last summer of his life : —

LANCASTER, N.H., July 3, 1877.

Dear Mrs. W.,— I am well rested, and I long for my regular work, which is a large part of my happiness. Pleasant occupation that goes "with the grain," and not too much of it, is a blessed boon for a man or a woman.

Already we had many prized tokens of your friendship, which we never see without lively pleasure; and such symbols help me when I am sad, by at once reproving and cheering a self-distrustful fellow who needs indirect assurances that he is not "a cumberer of the ground." I am very grateful for my friendships, only wishing that I could give as much as I get for them.

I am glad you find so many lovers of your brain children in the West, although I knew it would be so. The West is full of bright people, who have a hearty welcome for every good thing, and the sectional jealousies, both ways, are pitiable. I am often asked, "Which do you like best, East or West?" and my answer is uniformly sincere, if evasive: "One star differeth from another star in glory."

DETROIT, July 19, 1877.

Dear Mrs. W.,— My sister Annie died on Monday, and I came to the funeral service. The burial took place yesterday, not long before sunset. She was a person of great intelligence and refinement, who loved much and was much beloved. Thirty years of suffering and privation did not spoil her sweetness or shake her faith.

I was at the Milton cemetery, last Friday, with Lizzie and Mr. T., to look at our half-lot, which is only about fifty feet from yours. It was very beautiful there. Your lot never seemed more lovely. I read the mottoes on the stone at Minnie's grave, although I know them "by heart" indeed.

PETERBORO, N.H., Sunday Morning, Aug. 12, 1877.

Dear Mrs. W.,— I am staying with the Morisons, at George's farm-house, about three miles from the village, and overlooking most of the region round about, excepting old Monadnock and a few other mountains, to which we look up reverently. I am to preach here to-day, as a "labor of love" to the parish,— the minister being off on his vacation. Nature preaches so eloquently now that I almost wonder at their caring to submit to the intrusion of human voices upon their attention.

We like our new house more and more. It is at least as pleasant and convenient as persons in our circumstances can reasonably ask for, and I hope we shall be very happy in it. It was always pleasant at the old place, but I am thoroughly converted to the new one. Edgar is nearly as large as I am now, and carries his musket manfully in the Highland Battalion. We are great friends, as we ought to be.

To his son, who was spending the week in East Gloucester, he wrote : —

BOSTON, Wednesday, Aug. 22, 1877.

Dear Edgar,— Your card to your mother has just come, although it was written on Sunday !

Slow mails, or males, perhaps, aged nearly fifteen !

I was at Cohasset, Sunday, where I could see Cape Ann through a glass; but I could not distinguish Mr. R.'s house nor any of its inmates.

Aug. 23.

Probably you will come back to-morrow or Saturday. It will be hard to leave the sea-shore and pleasant friends, but we all have to do such things now and then. It must have been beautiful on the rocks, last evening.

Aug. 25.

I have just telegraphed that you may stay until the Monday boat. We shall be very glad to have you at home again. It will be sixteen years, Monday, since your mother and I were married, and you ought to be willing to spend a part of the day with us. I have no doubt that you are, and that you will come back "like a man."

Your affectionate father,
T. J. Mumford.

XI.

LAST HOURS.

Sunday morning, Aug. 26, found him early sitting on the piazza, enjoying the freshness of the hour and the gradual lighting up of the western hills. For the first time for many Sundays he did not attend public worship, but threw himself on the lounge for a morning nap, having as yet made no allusion to any pain. Several friends came to lunch, and some later to dine, so that the house was filled with guests till evening. Always of very genial manner, his hospitality assumed a playful mood, as he welcomed his friends, and showed them over the house, and took them out on the house-top, which commands a view of the surrounding country. At four o'clock he asked to be excused from table, and ascended the stairs for the last time. He was then suffering considerable pain, which did not cease till death released him. When, the next morning, the doctor told him he was a much sicker man than he had expected to find, he said, "If you will do all you can for me, doctor, I will be very grateful to you." To all who ministered to his wants he gave the gracious smile and the cordial "Thank you." He was never more considerate of the comfort of others than when they were bending over him to relieve him, being as submissive to their wishes as a little child.

His "boy," as he loved to call him, came back full of vigor and joyousness, to find his father on his bed of pain. Throwing his arms around his neck, he said, "Well, my dear boy, I am glad you've got home. There was a time, last night, when I thought I should never see my little boy again, but I am not suffering so much now. You don't know how I love you!"

The next morning a consultation of physicians was held, and

telegraphic messages were sent to his brothers and sister, and the friends whom he designated. He said to an attendant, " I must be very ill, if it is necessary to call another physician. I should like to live to see my boy grow up."

His mind was clear, and his thoughts busy, except for a few hours at the last.

The coming campaign and the coming issue of his paper were discussed by him in the intervals of comparative ease, and many recent interviews with friends were repeated, especially a conversation on immortality he had had with a friend, the week before, at Cohasset, where he last preached.

No direct reference to the impending change, no parting word, as such, was said; for to the last there was hope of recovery, and his loved ones did not wish to hinder it by the least exciting thought. His feelings and convictions about death and the immortal life were so well known, and so freely had he been accustomed to talk with his family in regard to them, that it would have seemed like an intrusion to disturb the quiet slumber into which he had fallen with any words of farewell, or to arouse him to the agony of parting. No one could feel more surely that in the midst of life we are in death.

From infancy he had been taught by his mother to regard life as a precious but passing gift. He would have been pleased to remain on earth a little longer, if it had been his Father's will; yet he was ready at any moment to go at his Father's call.

At five minutes past eight o'clock, Wednesday morning, August 29, just as the train which was accustomed to take him to town left the station, he passed "beyond the sighing and the weeping" into the "love, rest, and home" that awaited him on the other side.

MEMORIAL TRIBUTES.

MEMORIAL TRIBUTES.

XII.

FUNERAL SERVICES.

The announcement of Mr. Mumford's sudden death came like a thunderbolt to his multitude of friends. It found many of them, especially his clerical brethren, away from home, spending their summer vacation; yet the large number of ministers and laymen from near and far who hastened to pay the last honors to the deceased showed how widely he was known, and how deeply and tenderly he was loved.

At the new house on Alban Street, Dorchester, into which, with his family, he had so lately moved, and which promised them such an enjoyable home, the relatives of the family, the pall-bearers, and a few of the more intimate friends gathered, at ten o'clock, on Saturday morning, Sept. 1. The services, conducted by Rev. Rush R. Shippen, were fittingly brief and simple, consisting of the 23d Psalm, a prayer, and one of Mr. Mumford's favorite poems:—

> Our beloved have departed,
> While we tarry, heavy-hearted,
>   In the dreary, empty house.
> They have ended life's brief story,
> They have reached the home of glory;
>   Over death victorious.

> On we haste, to home invited,
> There with friends to be united
>   In a surer bond than here.
> Meeting soon, and met forever :
> Glorious hope, forsake us never,
>   For thy glimmering light is dear !

Ah! the way is shining clearer,
As we journey ever nearer
  To the everlasting home.
Comrades, who await our landing,
Friends, who round the throne are standing,
  We salute you, and we come.

By request of the members of the Third Religious Society, who wished to testify in some appropriate manner to the great love they bore their former pastor, public funeral services were held at their church on Richmond Street. Thither the casket was removed, where it was placed under the pulpit, on a dais surrounded with ferns and lilies, and covered with a wreath of ivy and forget-me-nots. The pulpit and organ were wreathed with flowers by loving friends.

The large congregation in the church embraced not only many ministers and laymen well known to the religious body of which Mr. Mumford was such a faithful representative, but many of different churches and faiths, who honored him for his catholicity of spirit, and for his eminent qualities as a citizen and a man; and there were many there who had known him as pastor and as friend, who had listened often to the devout and earnest words which fell from his lips as he stood in the sacred desk, or who, in the hour of bereavement, had known his rare power to counsel and console.

The solemn funeral march on the organ was followed by the sweet minor, "Come unto me, all ye that are heavy laden."

Rev. Henry G. Spaulding, his friend, and successor to the pastorate of the church, read a selection from the Scriptures; after which the choir, composed of nine young ladies, some of whom had the tenderest memories of his pastoral care, then sang the following hymn: —

We will not weep; for God is standing by us,
  And tears will blind us to the blessed sight.
We will not doubt; if darkness still doth try us,
  Our souls have promise of serenest light.

We will not faint; if heavy burdens bind us,
 They press no harder than our souls can bear.
The thorniest way is lying still behind us ;
 We shall be braver for the past despair.

Oh, not in doubt shall be our journey's ending !
 Sin, with its fears, shall leave us at the last ;
All its best hopes in glad fulfilment blending,
 Life shall be with us when the death is past.

Help us, O Father ! when the world is pressing
 On our frail hearts, that faint without their friend ;
Help us, O Father ! let thy constant blessing
 Strengthen our weakness, till the joyful end.

Rev. James Freeman Clarke, on the occasion of Mr. Mumford's settlement at Detroit, preached the ordination sermon, and had ever since remained his close and warm friend. It was fitting that he who had ushered him into the ministry should mark its close with a memorial word.

ADDRESS OF REV. JAMES FREEMAN CLARKE, D.D.

The large number who have been brought together, this morning, from places nearer or more remote, shows how deeply and how widely-felt is the sudden, sad bereavement which calls us here. Very many here, this morning, feel that they have lost a friend and a brother so near to them, on whom they have been so dependent, that this loss can never be replaced on earth. And many of us also, looking at the important place which our friend occupied in the community, his remarkable usefulness and his special adaptation to his work, must think that the place which he last filled can never be occupied again by any one so competent to that work. And then in our hearts, as so often, we look up and say, Why *he!* why *he!* Why not some of the rest of us, less useful, less needed, on whom fewer rely? Why are those taken that we can so ill-spare? We can answer nothing to that. There is only one answer to it. Faith only can answer it, which knows that these events do not come by any blind chance, or by any iron-clad law of destiny, but that they come according to the will, knowledge, and love of an Infinite Tenderness; and therefore, if we could see through it all, as God and the angels to-day see it, we should gladly and willingly accept it, and say it is all right, all good, and all for the best. I suppose that in the other world, as here, good and true and useful men are wanted, and that when they are taken from us in the midst of such great activity, leaving us in the prime of their life and in the full measure of their power, when they are accomplishing so much, they go not to rest, except to that rest which comes from fuller work and greater activity. Our dear brother goes on, but not to any idleness. There is a place waiting for him, ready for him, in some one of the many mansions of the house of the universal Father; and there he will once more put that untiring mind, that perfect affection and tender-ness, and that determined will to a new work in that higher world; but to us it is a loss, and a great one. He appeared to have found his place, where he could be so well-occupied during the many years that seemed to lie before him, full of fruit to be gathered by his untiring hand. Able

and worthy men have occupied the position which
he occupied ; and yet, somehow, he seemed to put
into that work, into the journal of which he was
chief, a power, a vitality, and a spirit which caused
that journal to become, during his time, better than
it ever was before. We all went in haste to get
each new number when it appeared, wondering what
new brightness and what new variety of thought and
appreciation we should find in it.

We cannot help thinking, to-day, of how much
there was in our dear brother. The passages of
Scripture just read, full of description of every
variety of human perfection, do not seem wholly
unsuited to this hour ; for with all our brother's
ready intelligence, all his ripe, keen wit, all his
sharp insight, his promptness of judgment, there
was also combined how much, as you know, of tenderness and the sweetness of a heart which loved
like a woman, joined with a strength of will which
made him one of the manliest of men! Not only
did he follow his great Master in all this, but he
also seemed to follow exactly in the footsteps of
that earthly master whom he so much loved and
esteemed. He was like Samuel J. May in uniting
with a woman's tenderness a man's unflinching
courage ; and therefore he was so dear to us all.
There may have been those who, seeing that active,
asserting power and insight, that sharp, discriminating wit, have thought that he spoke recklessly
sometimes, and was willing to wound his opponents; but those who knew him well knew it was

not in the least so. He said what he saw, and could not help saying it; but there never was one touch of bitterness or of unkindness in anything that came from the pen of our brother. Those who knew his heart knew that to be the truth.

And so, to-day, we say we have lost one of the bravest of men and the tenderest of friends. Not lost; no, not lost. Such powers, so exerted, remain with us always. Long as any of you shall live, you will never cease to have him with you. His love and his intelligence,—they will go with you always. But there is something more which we must not omit saying, now, in this church, where so many knew the deep religious feeling of our brother,— we must not omit saying that, joined with these other powers, there was a faith in God like that of a little child. I recollect one little incident which he spoke of more than once to me. One night we were walking together. It was a dark night, and we were going along a path which I knew very well, but which was unknown to him; and we came to several places where I said, "Take my hand now. I will lead you. This is a difficult place. Now, here, jump. It is all right; jump." And so he jumped, and so he would follow. And afterward he said that it seemed to him an emblem of the childlike faith we ought always to have : not only that he followed willingly, but that he followed gladly; and that there was a certain joy which he felt in leaping into the darkness, knowing that his friend was there, and could not make a mistake. And so, on a higher platform, he has repeated that little story when standing by the table of his Master, and urging upon you to trust God, and to trust his grace. In this spirit, too, with an ampler belief and reliance, he has gone to take what some doubters call another leap into the dark. But we know that there was no darkness to him there, and that when he found himself in that other world, with those new surroundings, he felt that it was all right and all good,— nothing dark, nothing uncertain. He was ready to go forward, holding the hand always of the Divinest of Friends, and trusting that he could be led nowhere that would not be for his highest good. He was ready to leap into any darkness, while holding the hand of his heavenly Father.

Rev. R. P. Stebbins, D.D., of Ithaca, who was President of Meadville Theological School when Mr. Mumford entered, followed with a warm tribute to his former pupil.

ADDRESS OF REV. RUFUS P. STEBBINS, D.D.

It is finished. The work of this active spirit here is done. I remember perfectly, as if it were but yesterday, when he came to Meadville a quarter of a century ago — having caught new views of the mercifulness of God and the brotherhood of man, to prepare himself for the Christian ministry — the brightness of that face, the ardor of that heart,

the warmth of that hand. From that hour to this,
and from this on, if God helps me to be as faithful
to the great work as he, forever on will our hearts
beat in sympathy of love. His name was always
spoken with warmest affection in my home; and
when I learned that one who was so precious to
me during so many years had passed on,— so full
of spirit, so full of vigor, so full of all the brightest
hopes and prospects here,— I could but wonder at
that divine Providence that had left me behind, the
shadows lengthening, the hands hanging down, the
feet faltering, and taken him, the strong, the vigorous, whose field was continually widening, whose
opportunities for usefulness were constantly increasing, and to whom we were all looking as a
great helper and a great supporter. I feel, friends,
that this is not an occasion for words. I have no
words in which I could express the strength of my
affection and the height of my admiration for our
departed brother and Christian friend in the ministry. I knew him well, and I knew him long; and
a more loving heart, a sweeter spirit, a more instan-
taneous judgment, I have never been acquainted
with. From the beginning of his studies, he continued to grow and grow and grow into everything
that is best and purest and strongest. And when
he used his pen instead of his tongue, how bright
was the stream that flowed! How clear, how pure!
I know there was no bitterness in that heart. It
was open to my inspection always. Folly and sham
could not pass the point of his sparkling spear with-

out being punctured; and folly and sham are always sensitive; but he never had any bitterness in his heart.

Within the last week he spoke to me something in regard to his work on the paper, and said it is best to have large freedom. It does us all good, he said, when we feel uneasy, to speak of it; and it does us all good, when we think we have something very important for the world to know, to be able to let the world know it: we feel better. "I do not fear," he said. "The good common sense and common, practical judgment, the warm love and charity of the people, will understand all this. And I do not think it is worth while for us to set ourselves up as popish and arbitrary; but let the word have free course as it comes to each." That was the spirit of our brother all the time. And yet, when a foolish thing was said, he could not let it pass without touching it with his Ithuriel spear; and if he did so, it was to show how exceedingly foolish it was, for he was wisdom,—practical wisdom. From the first day that he entered the Theological School at Meadville, all through his life, he was eminent for his practical wisdom. In nothing was he more noted, except for his loving, all-embracing sympathy and kindness.

But why do I speak? As the fragrance of these flowers fills the church, so the fragrance of his memory is in every heart, and is fresh in all our thoughts. Brethren, may God help us to be as faithful as our departed brother, so that when we shall pass on, others will cherish our memory, and honor and imitate our faithfulness!

HYMN.

"Oh for the peace that floweth as a river,
Making life's desert-places bloom and smile!
Oh for that faith to grasp the glad Forever,
Amid the shadows of earth's Little While !

" A little while, 'mid shadow and illusion,
To strive by faith love's mysteries to spell,
Then read each dark enigma's bright solution,
Then hail sight's verdict,— He doth all things well.

" And He who is Himself the Gift and Giver,
The future glory and the present smile,
With the bright promise of the glad Forever,
Will light the shadows of earth's Little While."

Rev. J. H. Morison, his near neighbor and friend at Milton, for whom Mr. Mumford always entertained the warmest love, added his testimony to the sweetness and worth of his character.

ADDRESS OF REV. J. H. MORISON, D.D.

My friends, the friends of Christian liberty and Christian truth, have lost a most able and intrepid champion of their cause. Almost every generous philanthropical enterprise has lost a faithful, able, generous supporter. As the chief of our principal religious paper here in New England, our friend was brought weekly into personal relations with a far larger audience than any other man in our denomination. It has been a matter of wonder to me to see how, week after week, he has met the severe requirements of this situation. We do not all of us know how great these responsibilities are. As the banker in his office, in trying times, is called upon at the instant to give his judgment on which other fortunes than his own depend,— as the general on the field of battle is obliged in an instant to issue orders on which the lives of thousands, and perhaps the liberty of the country, depend,— so the editor of a paper, in trying times, is often obliged at the moment to make up his mind, and issue his opinions, on subjects of vast interest to the whole community which he represents. It has been to me a matter of surprise, knowing the previous life of our friend, that he should understand so well as he did all the circumstances which must enter into such a judgment, so as to be able, week after week, to issue those extemporary opinions, so many of them, and very seldom one which did not commend itself to our judgment. Thus we have met with a great public loss, and we cannot tell how that loss may be supplied. But, in a time like this, we who have lived near him, we who have known him in the closer and dearer relations of life, look inward, and think of him as he was in himself, and as he was to us, — our neighbor, our brother, our friend. It seems but a little while since we gathered here in this church, to welcome him as a minister of Christ. It seems but a little while. He came heralded by no sounding of trumpets,—only by that very modest bearing of his; but year by year, and week by week, he was winning his way into the hearts of those who were around him, until at last it seemed to us as if our homes were worth more to us than they had been, because he sometimes came to us. The tenderness, the sweetness, the child-like trust in him, endeared him very much to those of us who lived near him. In looking forward to the possible trials that might fall upon us, the heavy cares which must in process of time come, it was something to feel that his tender sympathies would come in to soften the hardness of the stroke; it was something to feel that his genial and mighty faith would come there, to light up the darkness of the hour. And when these trials came, and this dear brother entered our homes so unobtrusively, we felt that his presence was a comfort, even more than we had anticipated. Sweet and pleasant and precious to many of us, to you and to me, are the memories of his kindly sympathy, at the trying moment, in times past. Dear and precious to us was our friend and brother. That is what I love to dwell upon now. Sudden, terribly sudden, we might say, was his death. I do not remember ever hearing an announcement of the kind that came more suddenly. But recently, in my native place, he had been to give a labor of love, as his custom was. Only three weeks ago he was there. Everybody was pleased to hear him; and suddenly, by telegraph, the news came that he had passed away. "Is it true?" asked our minister there, with tears in his eyes,—"is it

true that Mr. Mumford is dead? Can it be so?"
And yet, sudden as it has been to us, it was not, I
believe, entirely so to him. Hardly more than a
month ago a sweet sister of his, the feminine,
softened image of what was gentlest, strongest, and
best in him, was suddenly taken away, and he was
called to Detroit, the place where her life on earth
had ended; and there, with his heart subdued and
open to the influence of all tender associations, he
was brought into connection with those among
whom his earliest ministry had been passed; and,
on his way home, he visited other places where dear
friends were whom he delighted to meet. Under
these afflicting circumstances, it may seem to us as
if he had been making a valedictory journey,— a
farewell visit to those who had been very dear to
him in former years. He came back to resume his
labors and to enter into his home,— a new and
beautiful home, which had just been prepared for
him. In all this, may we not see the hand of a
loving Providence gently leading and preparing him
for the last change on earth,— the change from an
earthly to a heavenly home?

A few weeks ago, as he and those dearest to him
entered into their new home, they said, "We have
here a home for life: may we not also secure for
ourselves a home for death?" And in the quiet
Milton graveyard they secured a lot,— almost, one
might say, with a prevision of what was to come;
and in making this choice, he was led by the tender
affections of his nature. In that quiet cemetery

were buried some of his old parishioners who were
very dear to him.   There especially was one, a
young wife and mother, cut off in the blossoming
and promise of life,—one of the dearest lambs of
his flock.   And there, too, were buried a few of his
brother ministers who were dear to him : one
of his predecessors in this church,— a thoughtful
scholar, a kind neighbor, a courteous, Christian
gentleman, Francis Cunningham.   And there was
another friend of his, Joseph Angier, who by his
social gifts and his gift of song had endeared himself very much to his brethren.   And there, with
these older friends, was he to have his ashes rest
near those of our dearly-honored younger brother,
Francis Washburn,— that profound and reverent
theologian, that gifted, saintly man, who seemed
only to have begun to live here upon the earth
when his life was transferred to higher spheres.
These associations, I think, were what led our
brother to choose that spot as a final resting-place,
that the ashes of himself and his family might be
placed there.

Dear, sainted memories gather around me.   This
place where he ministered calls up the form of his
immediate predecessor, a devoted, faithful, Christian
man, who, greatly beloved and lamented, was called
away from his earthly labors.   But not with the
dead are we to dwell here.   Not in that cemetery,
beautiful as it is, and hallowed as are the associations connected with it,— not there does the thought
of our dear brother lead us.   A man so full of life,

so full of intelligence, so full of spiritual power,— it is hard to associate the thought of him with the grave. He has nothing to do with that. It is the *dust* that mingles with its kindred dust. Such a life is the strongest visible assurance that we can have of the immortal world; and it requires no effort of the imagination to transfer him there, but rather an effort to prevent it. No effort of the imagination is called for, to see him there, with the sweet and beautiful spirit of the sister who only a few weeks ago passed from earth to heaven,— to see him mingling with the many with whom he has been connected here, and carrying on with them, in higher forms of life, the work which was begun here. For, as has been said, all his friends were dear friends. Those who, by one of a less generous and a less loving nature, might have been looked upon as instruments for work were all his personal friends,— dear friends.

We cannot but think of him now as joining dear friends in that higher world, to rejoice with them, to work with them under the same blessed Father, under the guidance of the same beloved and revered Lord and Saviour to whom he had looked here with so much reverence and love. Yes, the limitations of this world are broken asunder; the separations which differences of opinion make here pass away. Even here, with all his severity of judgment on what seemed to him wrong, and with all the firmness with which he held to what he thought was the truth, he was very tolerant,— no, not tolerant, for tolerance implies some assumption of superiority, and he looked upon those who differed from him with a most catholic spirit, just as he looked on those who agreed with him, so far as they were personally concerned. They were his brethren, they were his friends, all the same. He was united to them by the same ties of confidence, affection, and love. And now, where I trust they all see more clearly than ever before, he has gone to unite with Christians of every name,— with the pure and the good of every name,— to unite with them, and rejoice with them, in "joy unspeakable and full of glory."

HYMN.

God giveth quietness at last!
The common way once more is passed,
From pleading tears and lingerings fond
To fuller life and love beyond.

Fold the wrapt soul in your embrace,
Dear ones familiar with the place!
While to the gentle greetings there
We answer here with murmured prayer.

O pure soul! from that far-off shore
Float some sweet song the waters o'er!
Our faith confirm, our fears dispel,
With the dear voice we loved so well!

The Rev. George W. Hosmer, of Newton, the first Unitarian preacher that Mr. Mumford ever heard, who gave him the charge at his ordination in Detroit, and who held a place in his affections second only to those in his own household, closed the service with a fervent, uplifting prayer.

The body was then removed to the cemetery in Milton, where, after a brief prayer by the Rev. Dr. Morison, it was committed to its final resting-place beneath the pines.

XIII.

BIOGRAPHICAL SKETCH.

For the number of *The Christian Register* next following Mr. Mumford's death, his friend, Rev. Rush R. Shippen, contributed as editorial, in substance, the following brief biographical sketch : —

Thomas James Mumford was born in Gillisonville, Beaufort District, South Carolina, June 26, 1826. His father had gone thither not long before, from Newport, R.I., but soon returned to the North, and died in early manhood. His mother, a Southerner, we remember as of quiet, refined, and gentle presence. Thomas, who, as he came to manhood, became, from principle, a foe to slavery, always cherished a certain romantic pride of his Southern birth, and a tender memory of the scenes and people of his Southern home. His later boyhood was spent in Waterloo, N.Y. Here he attended an excellent academy, studying Latin ; at seventeen delivering an oration on Ireland ; graduating at eighteen, noted for his bright promise ; and the same year giving the Fourth of July oration for the town. He then studied law ; but, following the natural bent of his best talent, soon turned editor of the county paper. After the nomination of Cass and Taylor as candidates for the Presidency, when the two great leading

parties of the country seemed to him committed to
the support of slavery, he promptly turned it into
an organ of the new party of freedom. He thereby
steadily, but with unflinching heroism and loyalty
to the cause he had with all his soul espoused,
in financial respects, ruined his paper; but he had
thrown himself into the forward movement of the
age, and its flooding tide bore him on to his best
experience and destiny. Coming to the Worcester
Free-soil Convention of 1848, he heard Charles
Sumner, and became acquainted with Judge Charles
Allen, whose friendship he ever after enjoyed. At
Waterloo was a little company of Progressive
Friends. Of this company was the family of
Thomas McClintock, who gave him liberal books,
and among them the works of Channing. Reading
these with avidity, he soon found himself outgrowing
the creed of the Episcopal Church, in which he had
been baptized and brought up; but, before he left
it, he applied himself to the study of the various
faiths of the different leading sects: and in leaving
the beliefs of his early years he broke no friendship, nor lost his loving regard for the church
from which he sorrowfully went out. Through his
Quaker friends he soon met Samuel J. May, of
the neighboring city of Syracuse. Congenial spirits,
with a wonderful spiritual likeness, they instantly
went to each other's hearts. Mr. May always play-
fully called him his son Timothy. They were like
boys together, with a warm intimacy closer than
that of brothers, lasting through life. And the

beautiful memoir of May is but a copy of impressions photographed on his young friend's heart. Under Mr. May's guidance, Mr. Mumford went, in the fall of 1849, to the Theological School at Meadville. Here he remained two years, having Scandlin and the Staples brothers among his companions; and as teachers, besides Dr. Stebbins and the other professors, Rev. James Freeman Clarke, who for recruiting health was resting for a year from his ministerial labors in Boston. There Thomas, as we must still call him,— for he always preferred this Quaker custom,— with his rosy face, fair as that of a young girl, his fresh, frank manner, his bubbling fun and flashing wit and fascinating sympathy, speedily captivated all hearts. It was beautiful to witness how, with superior culture, his quick sympathy saw, under the uncouth exterior of the sailor boy, just from the ship's deck and from Father Taylor's Bethel, the inner worth and nobility of Scandlin. Unlike as they were in training and experience, their hearts were kindred. The gracious spirit of Mumford was to Scandlin like sunshine to a flower.

At Meadville, as through life, he cared little for abstract studies of history, philosophy, or theology. Whatever he did in this direction was done from a sense of duty. But biography and poetry were his delight. From personal memoirs and diaries and correspondence, incident and anecdote and the lofty inspirations of song, he gathered spiritual food as a bee gathers honey. His memory was quick, accurate, and tenacious. He had also, from the first, the precision of expression, the grace and finish, that always characterized his writing. His prayers and extempore speeches manifested it. His sentences, whether in sermon, correspondence, or editorial, always fell at once from his pen just as they remained,— clear-cut and finished in expression.

His fondness for poetry and his enthusiasm for freedom became a new inspiration to the school. His fellow-students and boys in the Sunday-school were charmed with the kindling influence of his example, as from the ample stores already in his memory he delighted to repeat long passages from Coleridge, Wordsworth, and Shelley, the stirring strains for freedom of Lowell and Whittier, and the spirited hymns of Samuel Longfellow's new hymn-book. There still rings in our memory one of his favorite mottoes : —

> " It is the heart, and not the brain,
> That to the highest doth attain."

Into the debates of the school, too, he introduced a topic then comparatively new. With romantic ardor he became the champion of woman's equal right to education, to chance for work with just wages, to equitable tenure of property, and to representation by the ballot. This was the theme of one of his first and best essays.

Like his father May, he cared little for the technicalities of dogmatic theology, but desired then and always, with unreserved devotion, to consecrate himself an earnest apostle of human rights and brotherhood, of the fatherly love of God, and of all practical religion. Following the guidance of Furness, he was an appreciative student of the Gospels, and recognized Jesus as humanity's divinest leader. His essay at graduation was on " Christ the Light of the World. "

In July, 1851, he preached as candidate in Detroit. No Unitarian society had yet been gathered there, though a few earnest Unitarians were eagerly awaiting it, and a few sermons had been preached by the ministers of Buffalo and Chicago. After two or three Sundays he received a hearty call, with entire unanimity of the people, immediately accepted, and organized the church to whose ministry he was ordained. Rev. James Freeman Clarke preached the sermon, on the Unitarian belief ; Dr. Hosmer, of Buffalo, gave the charge; and Rev. Rush R. Shippen, of Chicago, the right hand of fellowship. In the spring-time he took to Detroit, as his young wife,. Sarah Shippen, of Meadville. Though she continued but two years longer on earth, the years were ever after rich with memories of their pleasant home.

In attempting to build a new church, the little band had subscribed their utmost, and were proud and happy in their independence, with the prospect of building for themselves, unaided, a new house of worship; but, as the walls were ready for the roof, a sudden storm prostrated them, and compelled the young minister, without Eastern reputation or acquaintance, to make his first visit among his brother-ministers on a begging expedition. Through

this trying ordeal he passed so bravely, yet so mod-
estly, that, while he accomplished his purpose, he
won golden opinions as well as contributions. He
never ceased to remember with gratitude his gracious reception by Ephraim Peabody, Starr King,
Calvin Lincoln, then Secretary of the American
Unitarian Association, and others. He at first felt
hurt by one brother accusing him of "speculating
upon Providence"; but, soon perceiving Mumford's
genuine quality, the same brother, with his accustomed self-accusing penitence, begged forgiveness,
and ended by helping him as generously as any.

In Detroit he remained about nine years, in a
successful ministry of unbroken affection with his
people, leaving only by the necessity of change for
renewed health. For a year he ministered to the
Unitarian church at Marietta, Ohio. Thence coming
to New England, he married Elizabeth G. Warren,
of Groton, who, with a son, named for Edgar Huidekoper, survives him, to whom go forth the abounding
gratitude and sympathy of a multitude of friends,
praying for the best consolations of Heaven to
sustain and bless. During the larger part of a year
he supplied the pulpit at Greenfield, while its patriotic minister, Rev. J. F. Moors, went as chaplain in
the army near New Orleans. While candidating for
a brief period, he had a glimpse of that trying experience, which he so graphically portrayed in a series
of articles in the *Monthly Journal.* Soon he settled
as pastor of the Third Church of Dorchester, and in
his new home at the Lower Mills village speedily

surrounded himself with a host of new friends. While here, he did good service as Secretary of the Sunday School Society, being immediate predecessor of James P. Walker. He became, at this time, a frequent contributor to the *Register;* then assistant editor; and nearly six years since he took entire charge of the paper, which till his death he continued with signal and increasing success.

It was a return to his first love,—a renewal of the boyish enthusiasm and joy of his first venture of manly work as editor. He always felt that in this direction lay his special gift. His style was terse, sententious, epigrammatic. His thought was too quick for lengthened, logical discourse. He disliked abstractions. He never fired into the air. He always wanted to see his mark, and to hit it at the first shot. His genius was as paragraphist, best seen in his "Brevities." To those who did not know him, his arrows sometimes seemed barbed; but no rankling wound could ever have been felt by any who knew the merry good humor with which his most pointed and pungent pleasantry was always sent forth. His fountain of fun and wit, perpetually bubbling and sparkling, was repressed by the proprieties of pulpit decorum. Therefore, though interested in pulpit themes, though reverent and devout, though attractive and effective in the pulpit, enjoying and never wholly leaving it, in the editor's chair he could more amply indulge his irrepressible vivacity, and in its opportunity he revelled with more abounding delight. He delighted in everything pertaining to the paper, enjoyed every number as a fresh flower, perpetually aspiring to make the next one better than the last. Nothing connected with it ever degenerated into mechanical routine. He was proud of the success of his contributors and of the skill of his publisher, and counted every correspondent and every compositor of type as a personal friend. It was throughout a labor of love. His work was a perpetual joy; yet few knew how laboriously he toiled. During the passing summer, many a morning found him at five o'clock writing his editorials. Many contributions he declined gracefully as he could, yet with courageous firmness. Meanwhile, he was casting his lines on every side, busy as a fisherman to catch the best. Through a wilderness of papers, dailies, and literary and religious weeklies, he wandered, to find the fresh flowers that made his fragrant and brilliant weekly bouquet.

With signal and increasing success, he made it the crowning work of his life. He was rapidly winning for it a front rank among the religious papers of the time, compelling for it the favor and respect of editors and readers of widely divergent faith. All readers discerned between its lines a manly strength and sweetness worth more than eloquent argument or brilliant wit. Behind its columns they recognized a Christian manhood that has rendered the paper less the organ of a sect than the expression of an earnest, consecrated soul. As the editorial chair became vacant, the liberal faith lost an accomplished advocate, and a great multitude tenderly mourned the departure of a most genial and loving personal friend.

Invitations to preach he often declined, lest he should stand in the way of some candidate, or of some brother who needed the stipend more than he. Though laborious Mondays demanded his utmost strength, whenever call came from a brother sick or disabled, for a pulpit service on Sunday, his labor of love was always ready. In time of sorrow to any of his friends, his swift sympathy was instantly at their side. His services in the sick chamber or at the funeral were unusually helpful and welcome, by his rare tenderness of sympathy, and by his quick perception of the fitting word for the hour. His affection willingly rendered them, however severe the cost to his strength, which his exacting editorial duties could ill spare.

His personal friendships were wonderful in their number, their variety, and their warmth. Generosity and kindliness sometimes hide unsuspected behind silent reserve, shrinking through delicacy from possible intrusiveness. Never intrusive, but with a gift for the expression of sympathy, and for establishing mutual confidence, he was welcomed into the most sacred privacy,— into the very holy of holies of many homes and hearts. The letters he wrote were like those of a lover. He remembered the birthdays, wedding-days, red-letter days of every sort, on the calendars of many a household. When not present in person, some gift of flower,

book, picture, or love-letter was sure to represent
him.   As his lavish outpouring of sympathy never
failed to bring loving response, we never entered a
home so filled as his with the unnumbered memen-
toes of personal affection.

None more sensitive to criticism than he; yet it
never swerved him, when the true course seemed
clear.   Nobody could use his columns for the purposes of personal advantage.   The generous appreciation so largely given his paper brought him deep
satisfaction; but in hours of criticism or of weari-
ness that sometimes came, would that he might have
heard the chorus of gratitude that sings his requiem!
Perhaps it cheers him now, as he already begins
some new service in the better world.

How suddenly he left us!   Yet how happy his
life's ending!   On Saturday at his post of duty, he
was busily discussing plans for the autumn's denominational campaign, and preparing material in advance
for the paper which was issued upon the morning
when we tenderly laid him in his grave.   On Sunday,
rejoicing in the rest and companionship of his
charming new home, he joyfully welcomed to it the
nearest companions of his daily toil, glad to show
them its countless tokens of loving remembrance,
and its lovely outlook on land and sea.   Then, as by
swift transition, he passed on to other loved companions and higher service in the house of many
mansions, the new home proving to be his beautiful
gate to heaven.

Farewell, O valiant soldier!   our knight without

fear and without reproach. Farewell, O faithful, loving soul, so gentle, yet so strong; so thoughtless of self; so generous to every human being; so earnest for truth; so loyal to the right, to duty, and to God! This world is richer and better for your having lived in it. How can we spare you from it? Yet God knows best, and heaven is more attractive by your presence.

XIV.

A MEMORIAL SERMON.

For more than a month it had been known that Rev. John W. Chadwick, of Brooklyn, N.Y., would preach to the Third Church of Dorchester, on Sunday, September 2; but none knew what his topic would be. How fitting it was that Mr. Chadwick should deliver, on that occasion, this faithful tribute to the memory of his friend will be seen from the peculiar circumstances which the address relates. Providence chose his theme for him. If he had searched throughout the pages of the written Word, he could not have found a more suitable text than he found in that noble life.

Mr. Chadwick prefaced his address by reading the following poem, by Henry Septimus Sutton:—

> How beautiful it is to be alive!—
> To wake each morn, as if the Maker's grace
> Did us afresh from nothingness derive,
> That we might sing, *How happy is our case,*
> *How beautiful it is to be alive!*
>
> To read in some good book, until we feel
> Love for the one who wrote it; then to kneel
> Close unto Him whose love our soul will shrive,
> While every moment's joy doth more reveal
> How beautiful it is to be alive.
>
> Rather to go without what might increase
> Our worldly standing than our souls deprive
> Of frequent speech with God, or than to cease
> To feel, through having lost our health and peace,
> How beautiful it is to be alive.

Not to forget, when pain and grief draw nigh,
Into the ocean of time past to dive
For memories of God's mercies; or to try
To bear all nobly, hoping still to cry,
How beautiful it is to be alive.

Thus ever, towards man's height of nobleness
Striving, some new progression to contrive,
Till, just as any other friend's, we press
Death's hand; and, having died, feel, none the less,
How beautiful it is to be alive.

Dear friends, for many weeks I have been looking forward to this day with joyfullest anticipations. It was to be the crown of my vacation's happiness. I was to spend it with my dear friend Mumford, in his beautiful new home. How merrily we should have sped the hours! What pleasant talk we should have had of nature, men, and books! How pleasant, too, the thought of speaking to his people,— *his* none the less because the official tie was sundered long ago. Once his, in any deep and earnest way, was to be his forever. He was to choose what I should preach to you. And has he not chosen? Living, he might have hesitated between this and that. Dying, he leaves to me no choice. All themes but one would be impertinent. Better be silent than to speak of anything but that which marshals every thought and feeling to its side. Better perhaps be silent than to *speak* of that. Better to sit in silence, and listen for the inward voice of memory and hope.

But we are under bonds of custom and affection *to* speak of our departed friend. The outer will not quench the inward voice. This will go sounding softly on, like music through a solemn ritual. This will have other days and weeks and years to hallow with his "real presence." Perhaps, if he could do so, he would lay a hushing finger on my lips. But from his interdict, might I not appeal to his example? How glad he always was to sound abroad the praise of noble men! It was a duty and a privilege which he had neither right nor disposition to forego. Shall we not try to deal with him as justly as he dealt with those who have, I think, forgiven him already for so frankly publishing their worth?

The story of his life has been already briefly told in the daily journals, and will be in his own with greater fulness by a loving hand; but you will gladly bear with me while I recount its principal events.

Thomas James Mumford was born in South Carolina, June 26, 1826, his father being Northern and his mother Southern born. In search of health, the man had found a wife into the bargain. Did the Palmetto State anticipate the recreancy of her son to her peculiar institution, that while yet a boy she drove him forth, like Abraham, not knowing whither he went? We might permit ourselves to fancy so; but a more rational explanation is at hand. The nullification days had found the father stanch and strong for "liberty and union, one and inseparable," and had convinced him that his growing family could be reared elsewhere more advantageously. The family life for some years now was more or less nomadic; but the boy was gathering strength and sweetness all the time. At length the roof-tree was set up at Waterloo, in central New York; and here, ere Thomas was yet twenty-one, he had studied law, and pleaded his first case, and lost it. Hence infinite disgust with the whole business, fortunately for him and all the rest of us. Behold him next an editor of the county paper, and cutting it away from its allegiance to the Whigs, to hoist the flag of the Free-soilers; going to Worcester to attend the first Free-soil Convention, and hearing there for the first time the voice of Sumner,— the voice of one crying in the wilderness, Prepare ye the way of the Lord, make his paths straight! If he was proud of anything, it was that then and there he gave himself, with utter consecration, to the cause of the down-trodden slave. How glad he was, only a few weeks ago, to celebrate the anniversary of that fateful day on which the nation's conscience took a new departure,— a small beginning of so many vast and wonderful conclusions! But while pro-slavery partisans were writing, " Stop my paper," another liberty than that of negro slaves was beginning to engage his thought, and other bonds than theirs. One of his anti-slavery friends was an equal enemy of theological and negro slavery. His earnestness was catching. The young man read his liberal books, and deeply pondered them. And pretty soon he made another great discovery: a star of the first magnitude, albeit

of softest radiance, in anti-slavery and liberal
Christian skies,— Samuel J. May, whom ever after
he regarded with a reverence second alone to that
he yielded to the Man of Nazareth.   And when this
good man died, it was an easy thing for Mumford to
write his life; for he had only to transcribe it from
the most secret tablets of his heart.   Anointed by
this prophet Samuel for a more than regal dignity,
the young man went to Meadville,— in what spirit his
honored teacher, Dr. Stebbins, told you yesterday.
Two years of earnest work and joy, and then — the
harvest being white, the laborers few, in the far
West of five-and-twenty years ago — he began his
ministry at Detroit.   There, for ten years, he did a
work of quite unusual spiritual significance.   His
outspoken anti-slavery gospel eliminated some of
his parishioners, but others liked it well; and
even among those who liked it least were some who
liked his courage, and could not resist the fascina-
tion of his gracious personality.   Very beautiful was
the influence that he exerted in those days.   For the
first time, young men and maidens found a preacher
who convinced them that the religious life is the
only life worth living,— the only life that has in it
any real poetry or beauty or romance.   Then, too,
the sorrow that had come into his own life made
him more fit to deal with kindred sorrows in the
lives of other men.   The gentle wife who came to
share his toil soon faded from his side, and left him
to pursue for many years a sorrowful and lonely way.

The Detroit ministry bravely ended, he went to Marietta for a year, preaching with good success, and adding many to his list of friends.

Again the lamp of love burned brightly in his home, and there was a little child set in the midst,— a fountain of perpetual solace and delight.

And then, one day, he came and preached to you. You heard him, and were glad, and he became your minister ; and all his happiness he shared with you, and all your sorrows and bereavements he made his own. How good it was to have him in your homes, illuminating them with his persistent cheerfulness and with his beautiful ideals of social and domestic life ! You know much better than you can be told what manner of life he lived among you for eight happy, blessed years. You have the record of them graven on your hearts. He remained your minister until his death, though formally he ended his relation with you several years ago, in 1872, and though another came to carry on his work with ample consecration.

But there came to him what seemed a wider opportunity. Had that early year of editorial experience bewitched him for all time? Possibly so. At any rate, you lost (from his official place) your minister, and *The Christian Register* found the editor for whom it had been waiting almost fifty years.

To those who knew him best, this abdication of the pulpit for the editorial chair must have appeared at least a doubtful venture. Not that they doubted

his ability to do the work appropriate to his new
position with sufficient skill; he had given proof
enough of this already, and of his liking for the
work; but here was a man who had a very special
fitness for the ministry, not only for its public offices,
but also for its more sacred and secluded trusts
of pastoral sympathy and consolation. It was as a
pastor, rather than as a preacher, that he made full
proof of his ministry; and herein there was no
cause of grief or shame to him. The necessity of
his nature corresponded with his sense of ideal fitness. He was what he would be. Setting as high
a value as any other man upon the ministrations of
the pulpit, he set a yet higher value on the friendship of the pastor with his people, his personal relations with them in their various joys and sorrows.
Who so glad as he before the marriage altar, so sympathetic with the joy of young hearts openly pledged
to mutual fidelities, or thrilling over the baptismal
font with the first joy of parentage? Who more in
awe than he of those "blithe go-betweens" who
wed anew our hearts with tenderer and yet stronger
bonds than those we weave at first? And who more
tender and consoling with the bereaved and broken-
hearted? Oh for such tenderness as his to soothe
us in our present sorrow! But in less formal and
more private ways than any of these sacraments of
love or birth or death "he went about doing good"
among his people. His genial presence radiated
hope and cheer. Well, then, might those who knew
him best, and knew the purity and sweetness of his

personal relations with his people, fear for him, lest his new position should oblige him to forego the use of some of his best gifts; and no doubt to some extent their fears were justified; but not entirely. "Once a bishop, always a bishop," say our Episcopalian friends. Once a minister, always a minister, was very true of him. There was never any abatement of his joy in pulpit preaching. As opportunities offered, he accepted them with manifest delight, the happier if, doing so, he could help some sick or jaded fellow-minister over a hard place. But the offices of pastoral service and of personal friendship were much less diminished by his new position than those of public preaching. His old parishioners and their children turned to him as naturally in their joy and sorrow as flowers turn to the sun; and he was always ready to respond. No doubt there was considerable abridgment of his immediate personal contact with his former people, for the new cares were terribly engrossing; but there was ample compensation for the loss in the awakening and use of other energies which had been long suppressed. All that was best in the old life was carried on into the new. No real friendship was allowed to languish; and for the new work he discovered a surprising fitness. Journalism is a sort of pitch which it is hard to touch without being defiled. But for him there was no defilement. The dishonest tricks by which many others seek to boost their journals into successful notoriety had for him no attractions. He never forgot to credit what he borrowed from his neighbors. He never promised publishers that their books would be favorably noticed. He never wrote an editorial with one eye to the truth, the other to his subscribers. His seed was conscience, and he reaped the fruit of joy. He seldom rested *from* his work; but no man ever rested *in* his work more perfectly. His labors never grew monotonous. Every fresh number of his paper was a fresh experience to him, to be made richer, if possible, than any of its predecessors. And how pleasant his relations were with all his various assistants! How proud he was of his publisher, his clerks, his forewoman, and his compositors,— living examples of his faith in women's wider usefulness! His sensibility was wonderful. Often the children's stories written or selected for the last page of the paper went to the printer moistened a little with his tears. I became one of his underworkmen immediately on his accession to the editorial chair, and never many days went by without some word from him, so warm, so bright, so full of health and cheer, that I cannot bear the thought of never getting another message from his hand.

I should convey a very wrong impression if I left you to suppose that there was no adulteration of his joy. Going his own way, he could not please everybody; but it was always hard for him to wound another. The fear of having been or seemed unjust would keep him from his rest until the morning broke. That incisive wit of his was, as he knew, a dangerous weapon. Often he thrust it back, half-

drawn, into its sheath. But how well it served us
in the day when some, who did not know in whom
they had believed, wanted a creed to flaunt at orthodox and infidel! His latest editorials were suggested
by some new appearance of this old denominational
ghost; only he shrank from the necessity of striking
at it through those for whom he had the tenderest
personal regard. "But I shall do it, all the same,"
he said to me, only a week ago. Small fear that
he would put their love for him in jeopardy; for
I have never found him so loving and so lovable
in all personal relations as when I have been placed
in frankest opposition to his editorial convictions.
There he stood. So help him God, he could no
otherwise. But his affections overleaped the line
of his convictions, and laughed a friendly challenge
in the face of men whom he opposed with all the
weapons of his wit and argument.

The essential quality of his work as editor of *The
Christian Register* was just what it had been as a
preacher of liberal Christianity. He was a preacher
still,—only he preached, like the first preacher of
Christianity, sitting instead of standing, and to an
audience of many thousands instead of to a few hundreds; and the sermons were his own earnest editorials, and the best essays, letters, and discussions
he could get his busiest friends to write. How
magnetic he was to the best things of contemporary
literature, secular or religious, sermons or hymns or
stories,—whatever had the step of progress or the
ring of health! He never tried to make his paper

more popular by making it less religious. The more religious the better, so that it was living and human. Who can estimate the good that came, and will yet come, of so much faithfulness and earnestness? "How far that little candle throws its beams!" His sweetest comfort was to think that what he wrote and brought together was read in hundreds of homes where there was little else to read. We who are gathered here are not a tithe of all his people. They are scattered East and West, all over this whole land. Thousands of men and women, and of little children, if they knew to what extent the paper was the coinage of his heart and brain, would feel with us to-day that they have lost a friend of rarest worth.

A week ago, all this, and promise of indefinite continuance, and now a silence and a void! Vacant the office-chair! Idle the busy pen which

> ... "never wrote a flattery,
> Nor signed the page that registered a lie."

The last editorial is written; the last breezy paragraph; the last sparkling "Brevity." So soon he follows the beloved sister, that it is as if she lingered on the threshold of the heavenly house, and held the door ajar, dreading to go alone into the ineffable mystery. I cannot make him dead. He was so full of life that it is quite impossible to think of him and death together. I have never thought of him as dying, but I have thought a hundred times of his old age,—how beautiful it would be; what a store of precious memories he was laying up for it; how he would tell the children yet unborn of the great anti-slavery struggle,—"all of which he saw, and part of which he was"; of Garrison and May, and of the heroes of religious liberty whom he had known and loved; of Furness and Lucretia Mott, Bartol and Clarke, and many another,—for our friend had an abounding faith in persons as the forces by which ideas are embodied in society. He had great capacity for hero-worship, and thought he knew some heroes in the flesh. It was his faith in persons that made the personality of Jesus such a vital factor in his personal experience. Except Dr. Furness, I have never known another person to whom Jesus was so real,—and I might add, perhaps, or so ideal. Historical or not, the Jesus of his thoughts was altogether human, merciful and loving, strong and just; and, cherishing this gracious image, he grew more and more into its likeness.

Hard as it is to have him go so soon, this sudden loss is not without its compensations. Who knows but that the sure decay of age would have so blurred his mental aspect that we should have forgotten what he was when at the top of his condition? Now, when we think of him, it will be always at his best. This is the privilege of those who perish with their natural force yet unabated. Moreover, in this sudden, swift transition of a life equipped for every noblest exercise of good, is there not hint and prophecy, if not convincing argument, of the immortal life! That God can spare our friend from this earth-mote that floats across his sky I can conceive, although I cannot think of any man to fill his place; but I cannot conceive that God can spare so good a workman from his universe. Somewhere in that I think, and seem to know, that our dear friend will gird himself ere long for service in the one great battle that in all worlds is always going on between the darkness and the light, the evil and the good.

I have been told that on a gravestone in Mount Auburn it is written, "She was *so* pleasant." "He was so pleasant" might be graven upon his, and be a better epitaph than the majority. Many a time have I been up his winding stair for nothing but to see his kindly face and get his happy greeting. But for all his pleasantness, there was no lack in him of sterling manliness. He was no genial optimist, dulled by his own security to all the sin and sorrow of the world. Only he knew he did not fight a losing battle, and that he was enrolled with all the best of all the ages. In many ways, I know the world is better for his life. I also know that it is happier and better upon this account, if on no other. Who could resist the fine contagion of his cheerfulness?

A lover of all truth, a friend of all good causes, there was one thing more characteristic of our friend than any other: he had a genius for friendship. Friends,— men and women, young and old, black and white, orthodox and heterodox,— he had them by the dozen. He knew their birthdays, and remembered them with simple gifts and letters, sweet and

wise. How loyal he was to them,— once, I know,
blazing right out at some fine lady's table when
one of them was lightly spoken of! Nursed in the
anti-slavery cradle, he knew the art of righteous
indignation. For all his sunny foliage, there was
no lack of toughness in his grain.

There is a presence into which I may not follow
him. If he had a genius for friendship, I think he
had a rarer genius for domestic love. Parents, wife,
brothers, sisters, child,— these were the chords of
his experience that gave out the sweetest music.
He used to write their birthdays, and the days of
their re-birth into the life to come, upon his letters
to me, as saints' days quite as good as any that the
calendar can show. He used to speak of them with
glistening eyes and accents softly hushed. And so
it was, although I knew him well, I came to feel that
I had never got beyond the outer temple of his
spirit, and that there was an inner temple very calm
and holy, sacred to the most close and beautiful
affections of his heart.

So much engrossed in his official cares, we might
have pardoned him if he had been forgetful of a
hundred little things on which the pleasantness of
life depends. But of these things he was not forgetful; he attended to them as if he were a man
of leisure. God does not always spoil his tools in
using them. Here was one with which he cut off
many a parasitic growth, and hewed a broader path
through theological obstructions, where two, though
not agreed, might walk together and abreast. But

in the process it lost nothing of the keenness of
its edge, the temper of its metal. The man—the
father, husband, brother, friend—was never swamped
by the official minister or editor. A purely business
relation with others, or of employer and employed,
was never to his taste. As soon as possible he converted it into something better,—something less
mechanical and more human. If it be true that a
great business is a great machine, he never could
have run a great business. Clerks and assistants
without individuality?—mere cogs in a wheel? He
never could have suffered any such relation between
himself and others.

There are many would-be religious people who
have a good deal of piety but no morality, and others
who have much morality and very little piety. But
in him the poles of piety and morality both appeared.
A righteous man, he did not save his conscience up
for great occasions, but put it into every least detail
of his habitual work. For every item in his paper,
due credit must be given. Not a word must be
changed in a contributor's article without his consent. He ventured upon no improvements, either
of theology or style. He was a righteous man, and
he was a constant worshipper. He did not save
his worship up for great occasions, any more than
his conscience; it was the natural pulsation of his
heart, responding to the daily beauty of the world,
the tenderness of flowers, the green of grass and
trees, the splendors of the mountains and the stars,
the faces of the men and women whom he loved.

I trust that I have named aright some of the more salient characteristics of our friend. But salient is not the word. Nothing stuck out. His various traits were all harmoniously blended into a living unity. A certain falseness naturally attaches to any analysis of such a character as his: the whole is greater than the sum of all its parts. All our analysis is made ashamed, as we recall the vital synthesis which was the man who loved us,—whom we knew and loved so well.

If any one should say, " Yes, but he had his faults, like all the rest of us," I surely should not contradict him. Doubtless he had, and some of them I could perhaps enumerate. Now and then, his lively wit got the better of his discretion. The wonder was, it didn't do it oftener. Considering the metal of the beast, he kept her well in hand; she didn't often run away with him. Many a witty brevity was sacrificed, lest it should hurt the victim more than it would help the truth. The last time I saw him, two or three days before his death, it was with the gleam of one of these suppressed brevities in his merry eye. But sometimes his righteous indignation left him no resource but, like his Master in the desecrated temple, to peel the culprit's shoulders with the toughest whip that he could braid of all his sinewy gifts of ridicule and scorn. Should any say, " But his judgments were often erroneous," I should answer, No, not *often;* very seldom, when we consider of how many things he had to judge. And where it seemed to me his judgment faltered most, it was because the ineffable joy, which his spiritual emancipation up to a certain point awakened in his heart, held him forever in that first estate of freedom, and did not permit him to achieve a freedom more complete.

But why should I apologize for him who was so good and true, so brave and sweet, and whom a friendly word could turn at once from any course where conscience did not drive him on? Let us thank God, dear friends, that we have known and loved so good and great a friend, and that he gave us of his love so largely in return. Sorrowing most of all that we shall see his face no more, let us remember well the gracious beauty of his life, and try to win a kindred beauty for our own. And let us show our gratitude to him by doing kindly offices for those he loved the most,—in comforting each other by recalling all his pleasant ways and his "hope full of immortality"; by new fidelity to every cause that makes for human good. O friends! it will be better with us till the very end, if any end there be, that we have had this dear companion.

> "O days and hours! your work is this:
> To hold us *in* our proper place,
> A little while from his embrace,
> For fuller gain of after bliss.
>
> "That out of distance may ensue
> Desire of nearness doubly sweet;
> And unto meeting, when we meet,
> Delight a hundred-fold accrue."

XV.

PERSONAL TRIBUTES.

The poem and papers which follow were printed in *The Christian Register* shortly after Mr. Mumford's death, and are reproduced without material change: —

LIFTED UP.

O spirit so gentle and strong,
　And fair with an honor unpriced !
So swerveless to shadow of wrong,
　Yet kind with the kindness of Christ !

O heart great with brotherly love !
　O thought swift with help and with cheer !
O life hidden holy above,
　Yet lowly and diligent here !

O friend whom no moment did miss,
　Of need, where thy comfort could be !
What hand shall uphold us in this,
　And who shall console us for thee ?

We follow.　We follow, and go
　Where the Saviour went up with the three,
And the glory of heaven did show
　On the mountain in Galilee.

And, living, we see thee stand,
  As Elijah and Moses stood,
At the living Lord's right hand,
  In the shining of angelhood.

And we know that the hills of God
  Slope down from their uppermost height,
With the pathways, messenger-trod,
  Into our sorrow and night.

O spirit most gentle and strong,
  Most ready with service unpriced!
Brave for us against our own wrong,
  And kind with the kindness of Christ!

Great heart, and pure life, and swift thought!
  Ye do kindle and move for us yet!
The friendship that earth hath so wrought
  Eternity will not forget!

No moment thy comfort shall miss,—
  No need, where thy comfort can be!
Thy love holdeth steadfast through this,—
  Thyself shall console us for thee!

                          A. D. T. WHITNEY.

It hints the immortality of character, that we first,
over one's mortal remains, try to figure completely to
ourselves what sort of a man he was. As his body
lies in its coffin, his soul sits for its photograph. We
are instructed by any distinct impression of a fellow-
creature; but no human being in life can confer

benefit beyond making the stamp of virtue and honor after he is gone. Our Brother Mumford will be remembered, by all who knew him, as a Christian without equivocation, and in whatever good meaning, above the articles of any creed that term may bear. He seemed to me always keeping himself clean from any taint in act or thought. His moral sense was ever in motion, sweeping the chambers of his heart of the dust which others, of conscience less nice, neither saw in him, nor might be conscious of in themselves. How humane he was, appeared, not only in his witness against slavery, but in his advocacy of what seemed to him the rights, and his indignation at all the wrongs, of mankind. I admired his earnestness, and the ethical heat which passes with sinners for ill-blood, but is only a spark of the wrath of God. He had a humor sometimes grim, almost, as that of Rabelais; but a heart of love throbbed under every stroke of arch banter and occasional touch of even biting wit. One's daily companions find him out ; and, beside the house he has left full, not of shadow, but of light, no official director was ever by his co-workers more liked. Indeed, his combined good-temper and prompt organizing facility would have fitted him for any station of chief importance in the duties of that supreme modern estate of the press. My testimony will not lose, if it have any worth, from the fact that on some vital matters of denominational wisdom and ecclesiastical dignity and discipline he differed with me in opinion, resisted my counsel, and went the way

which I have no question was pure and right to him,
his personal qualities always mightily backing his
editorial weight.   If his conviction, however, on any
point changed, I always in conversation found him
ready to confess it frankly and simply as a child.
There is no greater test of intellectual honesty and
a sweet disposition than to conduct a paper and
address a divided constituency about all partisan
and public affairs.   He is noble who can justly face
that vast audience commanded by the silent pen,
which is louder, to-day, than any gun.   Ingenuous
and unsoured in every word, he, that summoned us
so fairly, goes to his own account.

Cyrus A. Bartol.

The ancient Scots, when they passed the grave
of one honored and beloved, laid a stone upon the
grave; and so arose those cairns that make a touching feature of Scotland.   It is a sorrowful satisfaction
to bring my word of loving memory, and lay it upon
the grave of our dear Mr. Mumford.

He has been so rich a blessing to me that I love
to think of the circumstances, and the hand of Providence in them, which brought him to us.   He was
born in South Carolina.   Between thirty and forty
years ago, his family came and made their home in
Central New York.   The father's health was broken,
I suppose by the Southern climate, and he died
some thirty years ago.   Thomas was the eldest of

the little band of brothers and sisters, and in beautiful fidelity he stood by his mother when his youth was opening into manhood. She was a sweet, saintly woman; and Thomas, at twenty-one, was husband and son to her, and father and brother to the little ones. He was helpful in every way; and interesting it is to know that his rare genius as an editor broke out thus early, and he became the editor of the county paper published in Seneca Falls, N.Y.

Worshipping with his mother in the Episcopal church, he was very intimate in the family of the rector,— the venerable Mr. Wheeler. His mind was awake, and in his search for light he obtained some of Dr. Channing's writings on slavery. He read and pondered, and rose up an anti-slavery man. And then he read more of Channing's writings, and began to doubt about what he had supposed to be the pillar and ground of faith; and at this time, meeting with our saintly Samuel J. May, he was brought into new life, and at once began to leave the old, and seek the new. And now we see him at Buffalo, one Sunday morning, worshipping God for the first time with a Unitarian congregation, and listening to a Unitarian minister. Then he went to the Meadville Theological School, and then to Detroit as the minister of a new Unitarian church: and there he made his home; and there he lost his young wife; and there his mother and brothers and sisters came to him; and that sweet home of Detroit, there are many who will never forget.

The young parish grew in strength and grace,
loving their minister with rare devotedness. But
he labored too hard; his health suffered. He was
obliged to leave Detroit after eight years of apos-
tolic fidelity; and then he went to Marietta, Ohio, in
hope that a more southern climate would favor him :
but there, too, strength failed, and he came to New
England, to Dorchester, and then to the chair of *The
Christian Register.* His work is done.

> "Servant of God, well-done;
> Rest from thy loved employ."

Oh, how we shall miss this dear friend! He was so
loving, so sympathetic! With a rare tact he came
right into our hearts, with a sweet presence of cheer,
comfort, and inspiration. No other man I have ever
known gave himself to others as he did. When I
went to his house, after he was gone, I found that
the conductor of the car and laborers at the wayside
counted him their friend, and were all mourning his
departure. Said a poor man who had felt his goodness : "He was next to God and the Master."

How we all shall miss his weekly visit in *The
Christian Register*, coming with wise, cheery words,
witty brilliancies, loyalty to truth, knightly courage,
and generous, loving conciliation!

In all our churches, along the valleys and upon
the hills of New England, there will be a sense of
great loss. He moved among us with such unosten-
tatious simplicity that now we are surprised to find
how much we have lost. He was so earnest and

loving that men of all shades of opinion loved and trusted him.

At fifty-one, in the high noon of his beautiful ministry, he has gone from earth; but his sunset here is sunrise in blessed immortality. Death is swallowed up in life!

> "O spirit, freed from earth,
>   Rejoice: thy work is done!
> The weary world's beneath thy feet,
>   Thou brighter than the sun!"

GEORGE W. HOSMER.

In the year 1854, the Western Conference met at Louisville. The session was one of intense interest. Nearly all of the churches of the Conference were represented, some of them by large numbers. Many brethren from the East were also present; and seldom, if ever, was there a more delightful reunion of Unitarian Christians,— one marked by greater earnestness, profounder reverence, warmer love, heartier good-will. Our dear Brother Mumford was one of the delegates to the Conference. He was the guest of a true and noble Kentucky woman, who was more than delighted to welcome him to her home; for she was a lover of freedom, and she had learned with admiration of his whole-souled devotion to the great cause. Like him, too, she had been led by deep personal conviction from another church into the Unitarian communion. They were thus well-prepared, religiously as well as humanely, for thorough sympathy; and the first grasp of hands revealed each to the other as a true and enduring friend. Their friendship was at once marked and hallowed by fragrance, as of precious spikenard, through their union in a work of practical beneficence. She had recently emancipated and sent to Detroit a young man and woman, in whose welfare she requested him to be interested.

None that knew our brother need to be told how prompt his heart's response was to such a request, and how faithful he proved to the sacred trust. In such service his great, warm heart delighted; for he was not one of the kind who make ever so much of freedom and humanity in the abstract, and are quite indifferent to the freedom and happiness of individual men, but he rejoiced in making the ideal personally concrete and real.

How true he was to his high ideal,— how obedient, in little things, no less than in great, to the heavenly vision! How beautiful the union in him of sweetness and strength! " Strength and beauty are in thy sanctuary, O Lord!" How brave he was, and how gentle and tender,— firm as the firmest, and so loving! And how wise a man he was,— clear, keen, yet broad in thought, quick in insight, sound and well-balanced in judgment, just and catholic in spirit! Personally how magnetic, drawing to himself men of most varied temperaments and of widely-differing thought,— often drawing them close to himself at first meeting, and keeping them ever after near in fond and warm friendship.

It is the aim and boast of much of modern journalism that it is completely impersonal. The great
charm of the *Register* was that it was thoroughly
personal,— that it was pervaded, permeated in all
its departments, by a personality so living and so
genial that it made itself felt wherever manifested,
—whether in terse and pithy brevities, in keen comments, in witty rejoinders, in humorous pleasantries,
or in compact, thought-laden, weighty, but never
heavy editorials,—as the presence of a bright, strong,
helpful friend. It was the permeation of the paper
by this winning personality which made it, not only
interesting, but also dear, to so many of its readers.

> "Oh for the touch of a vanished hand !
> And the sound of a voice that is still."

To go one day to that editorial room, and see there
the radiant face and receive the warm grasp, and
on the next visit to find funereal crape on the closed
and locked door!— this is one of earth's saddest,
most startling experiences. It tells us, and most
impressively, of death ; but, thanks to the ever-living
God and his great revealings, it does not tell us of
our friend's death. Such a friend, so overflowing
with life, like Milton's angels, "vital in every part,"
cannot die. He cannot but live, and live forever,
and be forever earnestly and lovingly employed in
beneficent activity in some part of our Father's
house of many mansions.

JOHN H. HEYWOOD.

September 4, 1877.

It is not yet four days since his body was laid in the grave, where it must return to the dust as it was; and for those who intimately knew Thomas J. Mumford, and who fondly loved him, it cannot now be easy to do anything but sigh forth the ancient lament, Alas, my brother! in the tender privacy of a grief unspoken and unspeakable.

But it seems fitting indeed that a memorial service should be held in the columns of *The Christian Register*, so lately and so long the scene of his wise and faithful work.   Among his twenty thousand readers, a vast and widely-scattered multitude will count his death a personal bereavement, as well as a public loss, and will accept this number of the paper as permitting them to share, in some sort, the mournful privilege of being present at his funeral. This public testimonial to the dead becomes a most truly religious service to the living, since it enforces the lessons and consecrates the memory of a beautiful and useful life.   Let us unite in glorifying God who hath given such power unto men.

Now, too, the man — hitherto somewhat hidden behind the editor — comes out in full view, and we realize the personal qualities which made an impersonal work so rare and excellent ; for there was a subtle aroma in his spirit which constantly exhaled through these columns, and made the paper a welcome visitor to thousands of households, over and above its high value as a medium of intelligence, a messenger of truth, and a champion of righteousness.

It was the wish of Samuel J. May — whose biography by Mr. Mumford is one of our fountains of refreshment — that journalists might be ordained to their work like ministers of religion; and surely, in our friend's case, the substance of such ordination was not wanting: for he was born to the work, and prepared for it by the whole succession of his experiences. He loved it, and was happy in it. In it he lived and moved and had his being; yet without being narrowed thereby, since his sympathies ever grew more expansive, his vision more wide and clear, and his judgment of large world-affairs less and less limited by function and profession.

His weakest side was in over-appreciating his friends, and undervaluing himself. He once wrote to a friend, "I think I should trust you absolutely, even if you sometimes felt bound, by your love for me and for the truth and the right, to give me blows that draw blood. But when you *can* be encouraging, it helps me to overcome a morbid self-distrust which has dogged me through life,— sometimes nearly ruining me."

But he might well have gloried in his infirmities, for a divine strength was made perfect in weakness: his moral nature was like an immovable pillar at the centre of his being; his hatred of cowardice, impurity, falsehood, and dishonesty was the only hatred of which he was capable. If he sometimes hesitated to trust the verdict of his own faculties, he never hesitated to obey his conscience, regardless of cost;

and I never met a man who seemed more free from every sort of guile.

He was a good fighter against what he deemed to be evil, and he kept his weapons bright ; but every blow was for the good old cause of God and the right.   His paragraphs were sometimes thought prickly or severe ; but there was not a drop of venom or corrosive acid in his composition.   His sense of the ludicrous kept such close company with his love of truth and disgust at shams that he could never refrain from puncturing any bubble of pre-tence in literature or in society, in statesman or in churchman.   His wit sparkled like that of the dia-mond, because it must ; and it cut sharply like the diamond, for the same reason.   And who of us could now wish that these fine angles had been ground off to make him blandly commonplace, or smoothly round as a glass bead ?   Now that his day's work is done, it looks large and handsome.   He wrought for us all, and we are all his debtors.

Ah well ! our brave comrade-in-arms — a loyal soldier who knew but one Commander — has fallen on the field ; and what remains but that we close up the ranks and push on the battle, building his best monument in our hearts by our fresh vows of fidelity to the holy cause for which he gave his life ?

But he did not much believe in dying.   With almost womanly sensibility to every form of human sorrow, he had an inspired faculty of giving comfort, and looked straight through the transparent phantom we call Death, and saw beyond only Life, lengthening out and stretching away into an ever-lasting future. His passionate yearning for human love and spiritual fellowship seemed to find its highest satisfaction in looking to the time when he should go over to the majority, and find in the land immortal the gathering-place of friends.

He had no difficulty in calling God a person. He confidingly took the hand of Jesus as a noble elder brother, who could lead him to better acquaintance with the Father; and he was a devoted believer in what he called Unitarian Christianity, because it stood to him as the God-given charter of human freedom, the God-given revelation of pure reason, and the God-given pledge of everlasting, all-including, all-victorious love. For the final deliverance of humanity into the glorious liberty of the sons of God, and for the safety of his own soul, he had no misgiving; and we may be sure he has ventured away into the boundless mystery with the living faith of Christ in his heart,— "I am not alone, for the Father is with me."

CHARLES G. AMES.

GERMANTOWN, PA., Sept. 3, 1877.

It is in no spirit of eulogy that I speak of my friend, for I would not offend his modest spirit in death more than in life; yet the spontaneous incense of love that bursts forth at the mention of his name would have been so grateful to his affectionate heart that it cannot be wholly withheld

Admirable as were the pungency of his wit, his
clear good-sense, his command of language, he will
be most fondly remembered for his ample, tender,
human heart, which took to its sheltering folds the
obscure, despised, and self-forsaken.

Of so high-tone and pure a nature that some one
has said, "He has not left on the earth so good a
man as himself"; so little self-asserting that, though
"he never did the wrong thing, he was always as
meek and gentle as if he had"; stern in *self*-demand,
full of melting charity to others' weakness, boiling
with indignation at injustice to the helpless, forgiv-
ing of personal offence, the peer of all who were
manly, yet permeated with such sympathetic chiv-
alry that every woman was his friend, with his
genius for friendship,— one cannot think of him as
enjoying solitary bliss, or, by a change of worlds,
being separated from what was his native clime
here,— the loving, needing, human heart.

At times it seemed as if the wide-spread craving
for his sympathy in affliction was too severe a
drain on his tasked brain and busy life; but his
feet were always swift and his tender voice ready
for the mourner's call. Who that ever heard will
ever forget the appropriate hymn of his faithful
memory, or the rapt prayer in which time and sense
and woe vanished, and only the dutifulness of the
child and the Fatherliness of God remained?

Never satisfied with himself as a preacher, even
his humility was not proof against the happy retro-
spect of his devoted pastoral service.

His loss to our denomination as a journalist seems irremediable; for, with a sound Christian faith, he had a most catholic spirit, and was respected and beloved alike by radical and conservative. But his healthy, wholesome nature would be the first to rebuke our faint-heartedness, and to reverently say, "My Father's cup,— shall I not drink it? And, dear human friends, if there was any virtue in my life, let it blossom afresh from the dust in yours."

ELIZABETH P. CHANNING.

———

. . . It was a sad shock to learn of our Brother Mumford's death, that I have scarcely got over yet. He was so genuinely honest, so fair-minded, and so sweet in spirit! Strange that some misinterpreted his playful wit as having more gall than honey in it. It must have been because they only read him, and that occasionally. Those who were with him more knew better. Even I was with him enough to *know* it was a mistake. He was as lovely a man, of as modest a disposition, as gentle a spirit, and yet of as brave a heart, as ever I met. He was too merciful to be unjust, and too just to be unmerciful. The first time I ever saw him he was standing up in the Western Conference at Detroit, fifteen years ago, pleading in his quiet way for "death to slavery and mercy to the South"; and in that speech, while pleading for the poor slave, he spoke so kindly of the slaveholder as a victim of circumstances — to be pitied, rather than as a man to be hated — that

one brother was provoked to criticise him in no very
kind spirit or manner, as I thought.   I expected that
Mr. Mumford would rise, at the conclusion of this
attack, and retort rather severely; but was surprised
to find that he said not a word, only slightly bowing
his head and smiling genially, while the Conference
proceeded as if everybody were happy.   It was a
novel experience to a Southern Illinoisan, who had
been accustomed to the bitterest harangues for or
against slaveholders as a class ; but it was an experience that has helped me to be a wiser and less
harmful advocate of reform.   Brother Mumford was
looking much more pale and careworn then than
when, a little over a year since, I bade him farewell
at his office in Boston.   It seems but a little while
ago that we met for the first time in conference; it
was when Dr. Hosmer prayed, and Charles G. Ames
gave me the charge, and Mumford gave me that
warm right hand of fellowship to the Christian ministry, in the Unitarian church at Detroit, Sunday
evening, June 22, 1862; and now, of the men that
were in that Conference, as I recollect, Ichabod
Codding, another noble fellow, and Thomas J. Mumford are gone; and many more friends have since
then joined the innumerable throng.   It makes one
feel lonely to think of it.   But we will not say
good-night, hoping in some brighter clime to say
good-morning.

I have read the *Register* more regularly than any
other periodical for a dozen years, and in looking
over my scrap-books find that they are almost filled

with it. I have one book of the "Pleasantries," labelled "Medicine for Low Spirits," because they have been this to me very often.

JASPER L. DOUTHIT.

SHELBYVILLE, ILL., Nov. 8, 1877.

The character-portraits of Mr. Mumford in the *Register*, drawn by so many loving hands, have left little to be added by other friends, save perhaps to deepen some color here and there, or add some faint lines which may help to bring out the well-known features. Very fitly has our brother's wonderful *"genius for friendship"* been spoken of as the peculiar key to his character. A more faithful or truer friend I never knew.

"Kind with the kindness of Christ," he had the love which is greater than faith, stronger than hope, and more excellent than the best of "gifts." In my remembrance of him, I cannot separate this Christian love from the swift thought, the sound judgment, and the keen wit which were the marked traits of his intellect. Loving truth supremely, he saw the truth with the clear vision of love-anointed eyes. His penetrating analysis went almost unerringly to the heart of every subject on which he wrote, or of which he talked; while, with the ease of a skilful house-keeper, he swept away those unsightly cobwebs of sophistry that gather in most minds as profusely as their material emblems collect in our best rooms, when the air and the light have been even for a little while shut out.

And what other leader of our ranks has shown us as he has done how to reconcile those commonly conflicting elements of a steadfast devotion to one's sect or party on the one hand, and on the other that catholicity of judgment which is but another name for the sympathy of the intellect with truth in all its widest and farthest reaches? But here, also, his Christian love was the double magnet which kept him, like Wordsworth's "Skylark," —

"True to the kindred points of heaven and home."

No other force but this can hold the mind in that admirable poise wherein our friend always stood,— never drawn aside by chance suggestions from his chosen line of thought, and never forgetting that truth is looked at from many points of view, and action may often be approved of by us when we ourselves are restrained from engaging in it.

As truly as wittily did his friend Chadwick say of him that he had hewn a path through theological obstructions, where two, *though not agreed*, might walk together and abreast. Yet this skill had come to him from no looseness or vagueness of belief, and from no preference of an unchartered freedom over the truth that maketh free. The principle which he stood for, and which in him was so wonderfully incarnated that it gave us all a new revelation of that principle's worth, was that of Unitarian Christianity in its simplest and purest form. To him, as to Chan-

ning, Christianity was Christ. To be Christlike was
to be Christian. Christian faith meant Christian
discipleship; and Christian fellowship signified the
large and growing brotherhood of those whom in
his tenderest tones he was wont to call the "fol-
lowers of Jesus." And the Jesus whom he followed
was to him, not a human ideal, but a divine reality.
Had he been one of the twelve with the Master in
the flesh, he could have been none other than that
disciple whom Jesus loved; and the love would have
been mutually strong and deep.

I dwell upon this because it was my high privilege
as his successor in the ministry, and so his pastor, to
know our brother in some of the finest manifesta-
tions of this his inner life of Christian discipleship.
It made him the beloved pastor in his own active
ministry, and the sympathetic comforter in times of
trouble which he never ceased to be. It gave to his
utterance of the unique invocation so often used by
him, "*Dear* Father in heaven," a power to uplift and
console, such as only one in fullest sympathy with
the well-beloved Son could have exercised. It made
what are so often nothing but the formal observ-
ances of baptism and the Lord's supper, levers in
his hands to raise the heart to the highest planes
of Christian thought and feeling. Fully to portray
this rare and inspiring saintliness of soul, is a task
that even those who knew it best may well shrink
from attempting. Enough that it has blossomed to
sweeten the common air that human spirits breathe,

leaving behind its undying fragrance, while the bright consummate flower is transplanted to everlasting gardens.

HENRY G. SPAULDING.

No analysis of Mr. Mumford's quality as an editor or as a man is adequate which does not take in his intense hold on persons. He had almost a genius for fine appreciation of noble characters, and for loyalty to them. Virtue, truth, religion, were always incarnate in his thought, never abstract. He cared, perhaps, too little for logical processes and general speculations. His appeal was always to life, to spiritual experience, to the tests of character and result. He knew better than many of us how perilous it is in religion to run out the parallel of thought very far beyond that of life; how surely religious speculations unbalanced by spiritual experience become involved in vagueness, confusion, and contradiction. It was his constant habit to hold up a disputed view or practice to be tested in the light of the conviction or character of eminent and saintly men and women. He studied theology as it incarnated itself in noble lives. Not following authority blindly, he sought for truth where it seemed to him to have embodied itself most completely. Without believing in the infallibility of the Church, or of any body in the Church, the consensus of rational and reverent minds had great weight with him; and his intellectual humility

in the presence of religious genius, especially before
the wisdom of high Christian experience, was as
childlike as his hold on his own religious convictions was stalwart and manly. Presumption, brilliant and erratic guessing in religion, found little
favor with him, and met, sometimes, the puncturing
javelins of the same keen wit he kept also in hand
for perverse and stupid bigotry in his own religious
body or outside, and which he more especially re-
served for what seemed to him to be charlatanry
or moral crookedness, — if in religious transactions
or religious men, so much the more certain not to be
spared. He simply could not help having a keen
sense of what was sophistical, vaporous, and absurd;
and it was hard for him to forbear the shafts of his
playful but thoroughly sincere rebuke: though none
but those in constant intercourse with him knew
how often he forbore them. And when sophistry
seemed to him to cover moral defect or dereliction,
his sallies had a ring of indignant earnestness that
was positive and sometimes startling. Neither dig-
nities nor denominationalism stood in the way then
of his scathing bolt; nor could recognized position
nor ability persuade him to assent, or atone with
him for what he felt to be loose or morally oblique
methods or conduct. He bore persuasion manfully,
and stood his ground.

He never struck for the median line of religious
sentiment or influence. Under his conduct, the
Register never was a denominational organ, save as
the Unitarian public found and rejoiced to utilize a

spirit so sincerely and warmly in accord with its best traditions, tendencies, and aspirations.   His hearty loyalty to Unitarian Christianity was personal, not professional; the genuine product of his faith and sober judgment, not the accident or necessity of his position.   He could never be made to comprehend the necessity of any denominational strategy that was not also the dictate of his genuine Christian manhood.   You could be sure that what he advocated he believed in, and that. what he rebuked he personally dissented from.

Few among us were level-headed enough to escape his open or implied correction sometimes; and they were happy who soon learned that the argument he conveyed in a witty "Brevity" left him unembittered by the sally, and with as much intellectual respect and cordial good-feeling towards an opponent as though he had discharged a quarto at him.   His method of argument was by epigram and instance. In relation to this, he once described himself as a "one-barrelled man."   He loved to load and fire at will, without waiting for the whole intellectual line.

That Mr. Mumford's distrust of mere speculation and abstract reasoning, and his close-clinging hold on personalities and practical tests, limited his thought, — limited, sometimes, his intellectual sympathies,— is very likely.   He sometimes did not understand the intellectual processes, the logical necessities, that drove good men, on one side or the other, to extremes where he could not follow them.   His Christian faith was as firmly grounded in practical conviction as was his Unitarian distrust of prescribed methods and authoritative standards in religion. To say that he was sometimes unjust to those who advocated what he opposed, is simply to say that he was human; since no intellectual position has been found so broad as to obliterate, or greatly obscure, the fundamental limitations of a man's intellect and character.

But he never failed to appreciate and rejoice in downright earnestness, intellectual and moral, genuine religious sentiment, and manly character. His loyalty to noble friendship was entire, amounting, in some instances, to discipleship. Nor did this make him narrow or inhospitable to any claimant upon his esteem and affection. Neither tradition nor intellectual conviction kept the key of his affections and spiritual sympathies. His pantheon was always open, and new shrines were continually appearing in it. All worthy causes, all saintly characters, all heroic lives, had a place, and there was no challenge of intellectual shibboleths. His success as an editor was in large part the result of his genuineness and whole-heartedness as a man.

HENRY H. BARBER.

Many have been the tributes to the memory of T. J. Mumford, forming a garland woven by friendly and tender hands. Amid its evergreen I would place one leaf,— a leaf of gratitude to him as editor. This shall be my simple offering. To critical judgment,

he united such kindly feeling that when the former
laid on the shelf an article intended for his paper,
the latter made some pleasant suggestion with regard to the future. His rejection was no rebuff, his
denial had no brusqueness, his refusal held no dis-
couragement. Added to delicate consideration, was
a practical promptness which clothed even small
matters with certainty. Joined with very pleasant
personal recollections of one whose sudden with-
drawal from our visible sphere leaves there a permanent void, are these memories of his uniform
kindness,— memories which ever recall the faithful,
the courteous editor.   MARY BARTOL.

As I was away from the city and the State the
week Brother Mumford died, I did not hear a lisp of
his sickness even, until, returning Saturday evening,
I learned that he was dead and buried. It did not
seem possible. He was the last man to think of as
dying,— so full of superabundant life and joyousness.
But it was even so; and as I had missed the funeral
services, and the tender tributes which I knew were
paid to him then, I went to the cemetery in Milton,
the Tuesday after, to visit his grave.
    The place was already sacred. I knew the way.
It is a charming spot, unspoiled by art as yet.
There, in a little clump of pines, secluded and quiet,
I found the place of rest. I could not mistake it;
for, while there were no marks of fresh earth, there
were unmistakable marks of a fresh sorrow which

had touched many hearts. The grave had been covered first with a bed of evergreen. This soft and fragrant bed was again covered with flowers, rich and beautiful, which had not yet faded, though it was the third day after the burial. Probably they had been replenished from the memorial service, conducted so tenderly by Brother Chadwick on Sunday, and also by dear ones who "had gone to the grave to weep there" alone, and to lay the best symbol we have of "God's smile" on the buried dust. Over his breast was laid a flower-piece, with the inscription "In Memoriam" in small purple flowers on a white background; and at the head, lifted above the rest, a rare bouquet, with a white lily in the centre, and calla lilies strewed around. The whole was fringed with a white border of Nature's own weaving. It was not a grave, but a flower-bed; not the work of the undertaker, but of God and his angels in the ministry of human love. Oh, how still it was as I sat there! And yet it was not the stillness of death, but of life,—quiet, calm, sweet life. The still air was full of the sounds of insect life. The cricket was chirping his happy though monotonous content. Now and then a bird-note was heard, subdued and low, as if not wishing to disturb the sacred quiet. Away in the distance the happy voices of children were heard, mingling with the crowing of a cock,— telling of home-life and home-joy still going on, just as if nothing sad had happened. The gentle breeze playing on the twisted chords of the pine-leaf harps, set in every branch-window to catch it, made music as soft as the murmur of the distant sea. It was not a dirge. It was not funereal. It was low, peaceful, quieting, like the lullaby of a mother humming her child to rest. I looked up and saw the clear, blue sky through the restful branches, looking as serene as if conscious of nothing but life beneath its boundless dome. I looked down, and a large velvet-winged butterfly, not long out of its chrysalis, flew by between me and the flower-bed grave. I thought of the angel at the tomb, and of that word which changed sadness to gladness, " He is not here ; he is risen." Here was another angel at the tomb, silently whispering the same sweet assurance, as he flew by in his risen and glorified form. " Not here, but risen," this soft-winged angel of a fresh resurrection said, in that mother-tongue of the heart which needs no interpreter.

Why is it that everybody feels what so many have said, that they cannot think of Brother Mumford as dead ? Why, but just because he is not dead ? Why could I not think of him as lying beneath that bed of flowers ? Simply because he did not lie there ; only the chrysalis, out of which *he* had risen. I could think of him as standing at my side. I could see his smile, and almost feel the pressure of his hand ; but I could not see him in the grave, though loving hands had done all that affection and faith could to take all the old gloom away, and make it beautiful. He was not there,— only the " clothes lying." The grave was empty. Thank God it is

so! Terrible indeed would it be to *bury* a friend.
Sometimes, in the burning fever of grief, the dear
one gone does *seem* to be *buried*. Indeed, it often
takes more than three days for the loved one to
rise. But not till some angel rolls away the stone,
and sits upon it, saying to us, with the assurance
that only true angels of the resurrection, whether
natural or supernatural, can, "Not here, but risen,"
do we get any real comfort, or gain any real understanding of what Jesus meant when he said, "I go
away, *and come again.*" It is the *coming again* on
a higher plane that the soul craves. And is not
the craving answered? Do they not come to us,
not just as of old, but transfigured? Do they not
at times appear in our midst, the doors being shut,
walk with us on our way to some Emmaus of fond
memory, and talk with us till our hearts burn with
the old flame which made our communion with
them, while in the body, a joy? Do they not come
to us sometimes on the sea-shore of our daily toil,
and kindle "a fire of coals," without wood, to warm
us when wet and weary with our nets, inviting us
to dine on the products of an invisible and fathom-
less sea, talking to us of the flocks we are called of
God to feed, and asking us if we love them, repeating the question as true love always does, not because it doubts, but because it loves to be assured
again and again? Are not our "eyes opened" sometimes at the "breaking of bread" to see celestial
guests at the table? And though they may vanish
as quickly and mysteriously as they came, do they

not leave their benediction with us, and help us at least to look up, perchance to rise a little with them as they ascend?

Dear brother, we will not say farewell; for thou art not gone to stay. Thou wilt often "come again." If we miss thee, we shall find thee, too. With the inward sight we shall still see thee, and with the inward ear we shall still hear thy voice. Thy sunny face will still smile upon us as of old. Thy keen wit and rich humor, cleared now from every mote which, unconsciously to thyself, may have ever floated in it, will still cheer and enkindle us. Thy strong words for truth and right will help us to be strong and true; and thy wonderful power to comfort the human heart in its deepest needs, and to help bereaved ones feel that there is no death, will still help us all to feel that *thou* art not dead; that

> "The good and the true never die, never die;
> Though gone, they are here ever nigh, ever nigh."

WILLIAM P. TILDEN.

T. J. M.

Lines read at the unveiling of Mr. Mumford's picture in the chapel of the Third
Religious Society of Dorchester, June 26, 1878.

In life an honored name,
    Bright, without spot:
A memory revered,
    And unforgot,
When touched by death's cold hand.
    What better lot
Can man befall than this!
    A friend sincere,
Glad with our gladness,— quick
    With love to cheer
Our hearts when sad, and dry
    The mourner's tear.

He sleeps the sleep of peace.
    A noble life,
Crowned with unselfishness,
    Has ceased its strife;
For him no more this world
    With tumult rife.
He is at rest with God.
    Mourn we not, then,
Our loss, to him a gain.
    Rejoice we, when
We think of him who worked
    "Good-will to men."

A pastor, brother, friend,
    A Christian true,
The Master's steps he trod,
    His work to do;
And humbly followed Him
    Life's journey through.
May we him imitate,
    All evil shun;
That when, upon this earth
    Our course is run,
Like him, we too may hear
    The words "Well done."

N. M. SAFFORD.

XVI.

RESOLUTIONS.

At a meeting of the Directors of the Christian Register Association, held on Monday, Sept. 3, 1877, it was voted to put the following upon the records : —

The Directors of the Christian Register Association put upon record their deep feeling of personal grief at the death of Rev. Thomas J. Mumford, late editor of *The Christian Register*, and express their high appreciation of his fidelity in the discharge of his editorial duties, of his intellectual vigor and brightness, the versatility of his powers, his moral courage, fine perception of truth, and devout religious faith. During his connection with *The Christian Register* he has won the esteem and friendship of his associates by his uniform kindness and consideration, and rendered, both to the paper and the denomination, invaluable service. The universal sorrow at his death is a testimony on the part of the public of their appreciation of his editorial services and the worth of his personal character.

While thus feeling a personal sorrow at the death of our friend and associate, we also extend to his family our heart-felt sympathy in their anguish; and, while we would not intrude upon the sanctity of domestic grief, we with them find alleviation for our sorrow in the rich and sweet memories which cluster around his life, and the consolation and strengthening influences which come from that beautiful faith which he cherished and exemplified.

At a meeting of the Third Religious Society of Dorchester, held in Parish Hall, Wednesday, Aug. 29, 1877, the following resolutions were adopted : —

The members of this society, mindful of the fidelity with which our lamented friend fulfilled the high trusts committed to him in his pastoral and clerical relations, and also in the various and prominent positions to which he has been called, desire to express their marked recognition and appreciation of his worth; and they mourn his departure as that of a dear personal friend, and concur in the adoption of the following resolutions: —

Resolved, That the decease of Rev. Thomas J. Mumford, holding the pastorate of this parish for the period of eight years, and more recently engaged in the editorial charge of *The Christian Register*, in the full maturity of his powers and in the active discharge of clerical and literary duties, is an event which will be long and deeply mourned in this community; that the pre-eminence of his intellectual, moral, and social culture, his conscientious and unfailing devotion to Christian duty, the gentleness, kindness, and courtesy of his manners, the generous emotions of his heart, and the purity and virtues of his daily life have justly endeared him to us all.

Resolved, That in his intercourse in this community while engaged in the work of the ministry, and in the kindly charities of Christian life, honored far beyond the usual lot in the loving tenderness of friends and neighbors, we recall in more formal recognition his fervent zeal in his evangelical labors, and in the promotion of religious and moral improvement. Actuated by a devout and unselfish spirit, it was the purpose of his life to accomplish a large amount of useful labor, and his full share of that labor; and this mission of his life has been signally fulfilled. Liberal in his views, candid in discourse, compassionate in his feelings, his character was ennobled by a love of social order. Possessed in a remarkable degree of those sterling attributes of character which constitute a generous, courageous, high-minded man, conforming his will in harmonious relations with the will divine, and recognizing that will as the mandate of spiritual obligation,— to these were added those graces of character and that inspiring faith and fellowship which touched our hearts to holy issues and give to his death its touching pathos.

Resolved, That his integrity of thought and action, his love of the generous and true, his abiding sense of accountability to God, will oft recur to our minds as his familiar presence, and recall the sacred memory of his virtues and the hallowed influence of his example.

Resolved, That we tender our sympathy to the widow and family of the deceased. We commend them to the consolations of that hope in which the departed found assurance. There yet remains the memory of one whose life was pure, whose character was unsullied, whose end was peace, whose rest is hallowed in every heart in the consecration of the holiest love, and whose presence was to each and all a perpetual benediction.

Resolved, That these resolutions be entered on record, and a copy transmitted to the family of the deceased.

———

The following tribute of the First Congregational Unitarian Society of Detroit was adopted Sept. 9, 1877, and printed on a neat mourning card : —

Called upon to mourn the removal by death of the Rev. Thomas J. Mumford from the scene of his earthly labors, we, the First Congregational Unitarian Society of Detroit, bring, with saddened hearts, our tribute to his memory.

He was our first pastor, a pioneer in the cause of liberal Christianity in the West; and the good seed sown by him has brought forth abundantly to testify of his worth.

As a pastor he was earnest, zealous, self-sacrificing; an ever-ready guide, counsellor, and friend; ceaseless in his labors; rejoicing with those who rejoiced, and mourning with those who mourned; in all things a faithful minister of Him whose cause he served.

With deep affection we cherish the memory of his many virtues, his loving and unselfish spirit, which, in his life, so endeared him to all whose privilege it was to know him; and we place on record our high appreciation of the example he furnished of trusting faith, unswerving fidelity to truth, and an unspotted life.

To his sorrowing family, borne down with a double weight of grief in his removal when his presence as a comforter seemed peculiarly needed, we extend our loving sympathy.

A beautiful marble tablet has since been placed in the church to his memory, bearing the following lines from Chaucer : —

> " Rich he was in holy thought and work.
> Christ's lore and his apostles' twelve he taught:
> But first he followed it himself."

The Norfolk Conference held at Milton, Oct. 31, 1877, took the following action : —

Resolved, That the Norfolk Conference hereby expresses its sense of the high character and services of its departed friend and member, Thomas J. Mumford.

That it tenders to his widow and family this testimony of affection and respect, and its sympathy with them in their great bereavement; while thanking God with them for the noble tribute he gave to the value and blessing of the faith we hold.

XVII.

NOTICES OF THE PRESS.

By the sudden death of this most estimable and noble gentle-man, *The Christian Register*, which he has edited for the last five years, and the Unitarian body have met with an apparently irreparable loss. The pathos of his death is deepened by the fact that he had just completed and entered a beautiful new home in Dorchester, and was anticipating a great deal of pleasure from its high and lovely situation, commanding the most varied and delightful view that Eastern Massachusetts can afford.

Mr. Mumford became sole editor of *The Christian Register* in 1872. For two or three years before, he had been assistant editor, and in this capacity had done much to enliven the intolerable heaviness with which it had long been afflicted; but his assumption of the entire control of the paper was a signal for a complete renovation. From the start, his conduct of the paper was successful and even brilliant. His editorials, when they were nothing more, were short and sensible; but at their best they displayed a controversial skill, a moral energy, a flame of indignation, a happy humor, or a lively wit that made them a tremendous power for good. But Mr. Mumford's leading articles were not the only nor the principal factors in his editorial success. His column of Brevities was probably read more faithfully than any other. No wittier column could be found in any other paper, secular or religious. Moreover, Mr. Mumford had a positive genius for selecting matter for the different departments of his paper, and for calling to his assist-ance writers and correspondents after his own heart, and for assigning special tasks to those best fitted to perform them. When we consider that, in addition to all this, the different parts of the paper were always brought together into an artistic whole, it is no wonder that the subscription list steadily lengthened and the financial success of the paper was secured.

The theological position occupied by Mr. Mumford was about midway between the two extremes of the denomination. If he often gave offence to the more radical men, he quite as often gave offence to the more conservative. The general influence of his paper was undoubtedly more favorable to the rationalistic than to the supernatural Unitarians. The men he drew about him to assist him were mainly of the latter sort. He had no fault to find with anybody who remained inside the Unitarian or Christian boundaries; but never feeling these to be any limitation of his own freedom, he could not see why they should be to other men. The attempt to foist a creed upon the Unitarian Association was made soon after his accession to the editorial chair. It met with his determined opposition, and elicited some of the most brilliant sallies of his wit. Whenever this spectre has since reappeared, he has given it a very warm reception. As good a stroke of work as Mr. Mumford ever did was in attempting to set forth in its true light the claims of Humboldt College, or rather its financial manager, upon the sympathies of honest men. In the famous " Year-Book Controversy," he took a course which we regretted at the time, and see more reason to regret with every passing day; but we never doubted his entire sincerity, nor his devotion to what seemed to him the highest truth and good.

Mr. Mumford had been an able and successful minister for more than twenty years when he took charge of *The Christian Register* in 1872. Brought up as an Episcopalian, when about twenty years of age his anti-slavery sentiments introduced him to Samuel J. May, whom ever after he regarded as his spiritual father, cherishing for him a boundless reverence, and after his death preparing his biography with loving satisfaction. Studying at Meadville for two years, he left the school to take immediate charge of a new society starting in Detroit. Here he remained for ten years, building up a strong society, and forming friendships that have never been outgrown. Next he spent a year in Marietta, Ohio, and in 1864 took charge of the

Unitarian church at Dorchester Lower Mills. Always a clear, straightforward, and convincing preacher, it was as the per-sonal friend of his people that he attached himself to them most deeply. He had a wonderful sympathy and gift of conso-lation. Young people were strongly attracted to him. In all his personal relations, he was one of the pleasantest of men. No merrier companion could be found. Impatient of purely business relations with men and women, he made himself friends of all his various assistants in the publication of his paper. Few men among us have such a host of friends. He will be sadly missed by them, and hardly less so by the larger company who knew him only in his editorial capacity. With a singular gentleness and purity and feminine delicacy of char-acter, he united the most vigorous and stalwart attribute of manliness. The motto of the Chevalier Bayard might without flattery be graven on his monument: "Without fear and without reproach." — *J. W. C., in Inquirer.*

The Christian Register of September 8 is mostly a memo-rial of this wise and good man. It would be a vain thing for us to seek to add anything to what is there said. And yet we would fain set before our readers some slight portrait of him as he lives in our thought. He was a substantial man. He stood firmly on the ground. He walked with no wavering or unsteady gait. Seen from any point of view, there was an air of steadfastness about him. And this outward bearing did not belie the inward character. He was brave in defence of what he believed to be right; but his bravery was no sudden impulse. It was a part of the inherent strength and stead-fastness of the man. He was a person of strong convictions, and what he believed he steadfastly obeyed and followed. Duty was the law of his life. By that, most of all, he was brought into alliance with the infinite source of life. Hence there was no faltering when great emergencies were to be met and great responsibilities to be assumed. Though he was born in South Carolina, neither the accident of his birth, nor the endearing associations connected with it, nor his personal interests could make him for a moment hesitate to engage early and with all his might on the side of freedom in the great anti-slavery conflict. Born in the Episcopal Church, with feelings of strong personal attachment to some of its members, he yet gave it all up, and fearlessly cast in his lot with the advocates of an unpopular faith, when the truth, as God had enabled him to see it, demanded of him the sacrifice.

A stalwart, steadfast, brave man he was, quick to see and strong to follow the standard of right. And this steadfast strength was not confined to the demands of his moral nature. It entered into his whole being. It characterized all his faculties. He was a man of the most delicate sensibilities and affections. But they were as strong and steadfast as they were delicate and tender. "He had," one said, "a genius for friendship." The circle of his friends was enlarged every year. He seldom visited a new place without making new friends. Men were drawn towards him and bound to him sometimes by an attachment as vivid and romantic as that by which young men and women are drawn together for life. He was a public man. As a minister, and much more as an editor, he was connected with multitudes of people. But this larger life, which sometimes takes away the sense of personal relationship and merges the individual in the mass, with him never dulled the edge of his personal affections, but rather extended and intensified his friendships. No press of public duty made him forget the little attentions by which he could show how alive and active his personal feelings were. If he could not be with his friends to speak the word he wished to say, he remembered them none the less, and had especially the gift of writing just at the most important moment, and with just the words that were most grateful. For want of these timely and impromptu recognitions, how often are our most dearly cherished friendships allowed to cool!

And within a closer circle, the sweetness of his nature showed itself even more affectingly, and added more richly to his happiness. "If," says Mr. Chadwick, "he had a genius for friendship, I think he had a rarer genius for domestic love.

Parents, wife, brothers, sisters, child,— these were the chords
of his experience that gave out the sweetest music. He used
to write their birthdays, and the days of their re-birth into the
life to come, upon his letters to me as saints' days quite as
good as any that the calendar can show. He used to speak of
them with glistening eyes and accents softly hushed. And so
it was, although I knew him well, I came to feel that I had
never got beyond the outer temple of his spirit, and that there
was an inner temple very calm and holy, sacred to the most
close and beautiful affections of his heart."

This strong, faithful, tender-hearted man was, for nearly
six years, editor of *The Christian Register*, and no one has
ever better answered the many and varied requirements of
that difficult and important office. In addition to his greater
and finer qualities, he knew, as by instinct, everything that was
going on, and how to deal with new or old questions in the
light of reason and in the light that was thrown upon them by
passing events. His death is a serious loss to the Unitarian
denomination and to the whole Christian community, while it
has thrown a shadow on many a private home and heart.—
Unitarian Review.

What Paul would have said to young religious editors we
can only infer from what he said to young ministers. Whether
we consider the pulpit from which he speaks, the audience he
addresses, the influences he exerts, or the obligations laid upon
him by the nature of his work, we cannot see that the functions
of an ideal editor would be a whit behind those of the chief of
ministers. We have just been reading with extreme interest
the wise and discriminating words spoken at an editor's funeral. However accurately they portrayed the characteristics
of the man whose sudden death all so much lamented, they
certainly outlined well some of the most essential traits of the
true editor.

The Christian Register, of Boston, notwithstanding its sharp
thrusts at doctrines we hold a thousand times more dear than
it is possible for a man to hold mere negations, has for seven

years manifested increasing journalistic ability. In the treatment of matters which must be brought, in the editorial room, to the test of a cultivated taste, a sensitive conscience, sound judgment, and a broad, generous spirit, we had learned to admire it. The recent funeral of its editor, Rev. Thomas J. Mumford, after making due allowances for the halo of personal affection which encircled him, the denominational spirit, and what we may not invidiously term the Unitarian genius for eulogy, brought out in several of its utterances some things which not only editors but readers generally may profitably consider. According to the confession of all, we note that what was admirable in the paper was preëminently the character of its editor. Some of the memorial utterances made by his friends respecting him are worth repeating, if for no other reason, as suggesting some of the distinctive qualities of the true journalistic character. "One could discern," remarks his successor, "between the lines a manly strength and sweetness in the expression of an earnest, consecrated soul. He gathered incidents, anecdotes, and songs as a bee gathers honey. His memory was quick, accurate, tenacious. His style was uniformly precise, graceful, finished. He was conscious of his special gift for editing even while he was a successful pastor." His style is again characterized as "terse, sententious, epigrammatic." "He thought too quickly for lengthy logical discussions. He disliked abstractions. He aimed and hit. He put into his paper such vitality and spirit as always kept curiosity alive, wondering what new brightness or new variety of thought would next appear. Folly and sham his sharp but never bitter spear inevitably punctured. His work was his joy and his rest. He felt an enthusiasm for everybody and everything connected with the paper.—contributors, fellow-editors, and printers." "Who could resist the fine contagion of his cheerfulness? Yet his pathetic little children's stories, written or selected, often went to the printer moistened with his tears. Every number was full of his best self, his thought, his love, his life." "His editorial judgment, in the quick and right exercise of which as much depends as on crises in a banking-room or on the battle-field, seldom erred. He was uniformly firm in his editorial convictions, unmoved except by new light. He did not try to make his paper popular by making it less religious. His faith in God was simple, childlike. He dared to give himself pain by rigidly excluding what he deemed not best for the paper, no matter who wrote it. He treated contributors with invariably fine courtesy, but with unmistakable frankness and immutable verdicts. When weary of criticism at times, how he would have welcomed this flood of appreciation that his death opens. His reward is, after all, not in our, but in the Master's, 'Well done.' "

How much of this is exactly true, our entire want of personal acquaintance with Mr. Mumford makes it impossible for us to judge. But that it ought to be true of all of us editors of religious papers, there cannot be the shadow of a doubt. The very perfection of a picture so nearly impossible ought to make all readers charitable towards editors. It should afford to every one who aspires to the responsible position a more lofty ideal. It is a great thing to be a good editor.— *Advance.*

The Christian Register — the well-known organ of Boston Unitarianism — has lost the most accomplished editor it has had during the fifty-six years of its history. This is saying much ; for the *Register* has never been conducted by a second-rate man. But after according to each of the eminent men who were Mr. Mumford's predecessors the full honor due him, it remains true that no other man who ever occupied that chair had such a genius for editing as he. From the time he took full charge of the paper down to the week of his death, he made it a model religious journal. His shining qualities as an editor were a keen and almost unerring moral sense, a fine literary discrimination, delicate, we had almost written delicious, humor, and unflagging industry. With such traits, he soon made for himself a unique reputation in religious journalism, and his paper became a favorite with all

who admire cultivated Christian manliness, or relish graceful
wit. It was our pleasure to number Mr. Mumford among our
personal friends, and to know something of those characteristics which endeared him to a large circle of acquaintances.
He was one of the most genial and gentle of men; unobtrusive, but as well worth cultivating as any man we ever knew.
Religious journalism loses in him one of its most brilliant, at
the same time that he was one of its purest, models. The
Unitarian body suffers the loss of a man who, while he gave
it a literary service fully up to its best standards, contributed
to it the more needed support of unwavering adhesion to
sound Christian faith. His acquaintances will miss a cultivated, sincere, cordial friend; and his family will mourn a
husband and father of singular gentleness and devotion. For
ourselves, we feel that we shall miss him sorely, especially from
the columns of the *Register*, through which he infused such
a constant stream of "sweetness and light" that we dare not
hope any other man will succeed in doing more than make us
keenly conscious of his absence.— *I. M. A., in Universalist.*

We read with sincere sorrow, and hearty sympathy for a
deeply bereaved family, of the quite sudden death of Rev.
Thomas J. Mumford, the able editor of *The Christian Register.*
He falls in the full maturity of his intellectual powers,— only
a little more than fifty-one years of age. Mr. Mumford was a
man of excellent spirit, genial in temper, endearing himself by
constant acts of thoughtful kindness to all that came within
the circle of his friendship. He won from our pastors in
Dorchester their hearty respect and love, both himself and his
now greatly afflicted wife often mingling in their public services.
A Unitarian Christian from conviction, the latter term, with
him, ever received the strongest emphasis. He had little personal accord with those whose liberalism dismissed Christ out
of their faith, and warmly affiliated in Christian sympathy with
many of his brethren of the evangelical churches. As an
editor, he had a remarkable skill in seizing and condensing

the thoughts and incidents of the week. His column of editorial comments was unsurpassed by the work of any of the
editorial fraternity. Short, bright, apt, sometimes keen, and
occasionally, though rarely, having a sharp sting in them, these
comprehensive notes found often a wide circulation through
the press. We were very widely separated from each other
in our theological views and interpretations of Scripture; but
we were drawn to our brother editor in our personal intercourse by the irresistible force of his Christian temper. We
may not speak here of our appreciation of this loss to our
sadly afflicted friend who so suddenly finds herself alone in
life at a moment when its common enjoyment never was
richer, but prayerfully commend her "to God and the word
of his grace," whence alone can be found adequate support
and consolation in an hour of such utter earthly desolation.—
Zion's Herald.

The death of Mr. Mumford will be felt as a real loss by our
entire denomination; for outside of his wide circle of personal
friends, there are many hundreds of the readers of the *Register* who have long since learned to love him as the unknown
Christian man who always said the right thing at the right
time in the editorial columns of that paper. An intelligent
man in Olympia said, more than a year ago, "I always read
the *Register* clear through, and I think it the most ably
edited of any paper in the United States." As we knew Mr.
Mumford personally, and thought of his unpretending ways,
we naturally thought the remark quite extravagant. But from
that time till now, we have not been able to think of a paper
that we could say was certainly more ably edited than *The
Christian Register.* The column headed "Spirit of the
Press" showed a vast amount of wading through uninter-
esting matter, to select with a judgment well-nigh infallible
that which we would be glad to read. The column of "Brevities" showed real genius, and we doubt not was read more
than any column in the paper, except, perhaps, the "Religious

Intelligence." Mr. Mumford's wit was of the order that does not grow stale with time nor wear out with the using; and, better than all, it was ever used upon the side of humanity and practical righteousness. Though so far away, we join most sincerely in the mourning expressed in the *Register* just received; for we shall miss the strong, helpful word of this gifted brother every week for a long time. No one can fill his place.— *Unitarian Advocate.*

It is with deep regret that we are called upon to record the death of Rev. Thomas J. Mumford, editor of the Boston *Christian Register*, at his residence in Dorchester, on August 29. Possessed of a very unusual aptitude for journalism, and gifted especially with a brilliant wit (which its victims sometimes felt to verge on injustice), he was most successful in his editorial labors, and did much to increase the prosperity of the paper with which he was connected. It will be hard indeed to find a substitute so exceptionally skilled in the difficult art of "paragraphing." And it was his sunny, affectionate, and most lovable disposition, his warm and faithful heart, his utter innocence of any attempt to wound even when his love of fun tempted him into sallies decidedly aggravating to their objects, which endeared him to many, and will make him long and tenderly remembered. He was most constant and true in private friendship, as we have excellent cause to know. At our ordination on August 31, 1864, Mr. Mumford made the "ordaining prayer"; and we shall never forget the sweet fervor, simplicity, and beauty of his words, or the touching religiousness of his spirit. If the "laying-on of hands" by a true minister of Christ could indeed bring the Holy Ghost, we see not how we could ever have strayed so far from the fold. But no divergence of religious views ever cooled our mutual good-will; and it is with deep sorrow that we say good-by to one of the gentlest and best of humankind. — *Index.*

The announcement of the death, after a very brief illness, of Rev. Thomas J. Mumford, editor of *The Christian Register*,

has been received with feelings of deep grief by a large circle
of friends. His career as a journalist has been highly successful. He was a vigorous writer and a brilliant paragraphist.
Few have engaged in their editorial work with a higher aim or
more conscientious purpose to be faithful. He hated shams,
and his keen satire and sharp wit were often used to puncture
hypocrisy, pretence, and cant. Frank in the expression of his
own convictions, he maintained them with unyielding tenacity,
having in view the simple end of truth. He was a man of
deep religious convictions, in the largest and best sense of that
term, and was steadfast as a friend. The denomination which
he so ably represented will meet with a severe loss in his
death, for he had, in an unusual degree, the qualities which
combine to make an efficient editor. This is not the place to
speak in full of his character and labors. As a cherished
friend to whom we were endeared by a long and close attachment, we would here and now simply pay a passing tribute to
his memory and worth. He aimed to do his part worthily and
well. His heart was true, and his faith was strong. His was a
sincere, earnest, manly, and Christian life.— *Woman's Journal.*

The decease of Rev. Thomas J. Mumford, the editor of
The Christian Register, which occurred on Wednesday,
August 29, affects us as a public calamity. He had made a
record of editorial tact and ability that may justly be pro-
nounced brilliant. As a paragraphist — in which character
much is expected of the editor in these days — he had few
equals. His " Brevities " in the *Register* had given him a reputation far outside of denominational lines, as expressions of
sparkling wit, and also — a quality which does not always
accompany — of generous humor. He gave occasion for the
complaint on the part of his more staid brethren, of at times
lowering the dignity of journalism; but those who felt the
glow of his humorous sallies judged that they worthily embodied a moral purpose. He loved truth not less than particular truths. He hated pretence, and with a facile pen always

gave it a punctured wound. He was independent, with convictions of his own, which he asserted with resolute purpose. His death was very sudden. On Saturday, August 25, he was in his usual health. On the succeeding Wednesday, he had passed away. We shall sadly miss his easily identified utterances. Fortunate, indeed, will the *Register* be if it fills the large vacancy.— *Universalist.*

The *Inquirer* will be deeply touched by the very wide-spread sorrow caused by the sudden death of Mr. Mumford. One of the keenest of pens ceased its work when this truest and kindliest heart ceased to beat. That the noblest and fittest workers so often fall out of the ranks is that which makes one of the most impenetrable mysteries of death. It sometimes seems as though a wise general would hardly manage his forces so; and yet we see only a part of the field across which stretch the lines that are fighting the age-long campaign of light and darkness, of good and evil.

> " . . . We trust that somehow good
> Will be the final goal of ill ";

and if we believe that tears and evil and death are somehow the raw materials of which the better and the best will at last be made, sympathy for personal friends and relations, sorrow for our denominational loss, and an unfaltering courage to pick up and complete the work he loved and would have done,— these are what are left for us.— *Rev. M. J. Savage, in Inquirer.*

The last number of *The Christian Register* is devoted mainly to the reminiscences and memorial services of its late editor, Rev. T. J. Mumford. If the half that is said of him is true, he must have been a man of brilliant intellectual endowments, and of a most charming and lovable nature. He was certainly an excellent editor, and we can understand how highly he must have been appreciated by those who look at life from a Unitarian point of view. We have always found the *Register* to be one of the most interesting of our exchanges. It was animated with a bold, free, but kind spirit, and the Unitarians will not find it easy to replace him.— *New Jerusalem Messenger.*

Mr. Mumford was a man of remarkably gentle, unselfish, sympathetic temperament and winning manners. He had, as Sir Walter Scott describes it, "a genius for friendship." Years after his departure from Detroit, he was overwhelmed, on his casual visits here, not only by his former parishioners, but by old neighbors and acquaintances who remembered his kind ways, and pleasing speech, and helpful counsel. He was exceedingly agreeable in conversation, full of interesting anecdotes and reminiscences. Mr. Mumford's editorial writing was always courteous and dignified, and the column of brevities in his paper was charged with both pungent and genial humor. — *Detroit Daily Post.*

We regret to record the decease of Rev. T. J. Mumford, editor of *The Christian Register*, which occurred quite unexpectedly last week. Mr. Mumford entered the Unitarian ministry from the Episcopal Church, and his influence in his late sphere was conservative of the claims of faith in revealed religion. Widely as his views in religion differed from our own, *The Christian Register* under his lead has been one of the most enjoyable of our weekly exchanges. It may be as ably conducted by another hand, but it will be fortunate indeed if its readers do not for some time miss the shrewd sense and the always kindly and often witty utterance of the late editor.— *The Watchman.*

We have learned with profound regret that Mr. Mumford, the editor of *The Christian Register*, of Boston, U.S., died at the close of last month, suddenly, in the full prime of his life, and in the midst of his inestimable service to the Unitarian cause. We were hoping that we might have soon seen him on this side of the Atlantic, that we might pay him the tribute his ability, sincerity, and goodness richly deserved. Many of us know how invaluable have been his labors as editor for a series of years. His full sympathy with and defence of the Christian position of our denomination are well known. He now rests from his anxieties and labors.— *The Christian Life.*

He was a man of talent, bright, cheery, and genial, with the best of hearts and the purest and noblest of thoughts. Mr. Mumford edited the life of his early friend, Rev. Samuel J. May, and he was a zealous abolitionist. As an editor, Mr. Mumford was a success, and he loved his work and faced his responsibilities with much spirit and public devotion. Although Unitarian, he was not a one-idea man in religious matters, and recognized the good in all. He was a pure Christian, and he carried his professions into practice. His circle of friends was very extensive, and the sorrow at his sudden death is extremely great.— *Boston Journal of Commerce.*

Rev. Mr. Mumford, of Boston, whose sudden death was announced last week, was originally an Episcopalian. He studied theology at the Meadville Seminary, and preached for a few years, when he went into journalism, becoming first a contributor to and afterward editor of *The Christian Register*, the leading Unitarian paper of New England. Under his management, the *Register* became one of the best and ablest religious papers of the country; and his personal character was so high as to win from the most "evangelical" papers the phrase "Unitarian Christian" as applied to him. — *The Alliance.*

It is with surprise and great sorrow that we learn of the sudden death of the editor of *The Christian Register*, Rev.

Thomas J. Mumford. Though frequently having occasion to differ from him on doctrinal points, we always considered him one of the brightest, most courteous and accomplished of journalists. Multitudes whom he never knew in person will deeply mourn his loss. The *Register*, in his hands, has possessed a certain journalistic quality it will never quite have again. — *Advance.*

We were shocked to hear last week of the death of Rev. T. J. Mumford, the editor of our Tremont Place neighbor, *The Christian Register.* Mr. Mumford was at his desk on Saturday, the 25th ult.: on Saturday, the 1st inst., his body was carried to its burial. . . . Though his paper and ours were often obliged to differ stoutly on theological points, they never, we believe, quarrelled; and we always entertained the highest opinion of his editorial abilities. — *Congregationalist.*

We are glad to notice that nearly all of our contemporaries have paid well-deserved tributes to the memory of Rev. Thomas J. Mumford, late editor of *The Christian Register* (Unitarian), Boston. As an editor, Mr. Mumford won a well-deserved reputation. The *Register* will hardly find a successor able to fill his place, though such an event is much to be wished for, that our Unitarian friends may continue to have a truly representative journal.— *Christian Leader.*

The late Rev. Thomas J. Mumford, editor of *The Christian Register*, was a vigorous and able journalist, whose special ability was in writing paragraph notes on the editorial page. He worked on *The Christian Register* almost single-handed, but made it one of the most readable and valuable of our exchanges. The Unitarians will find it difficult to find an equally good manager for their chief denominational paper.— *Independent.*

From his childhood up, all distinctions of caste and condition were overborne by his respect and love for humanity. That last Sunday of his life, spent in his own home with its wide outlook upon earth and sea and sky, surrounded by his own household, and his friends and fellow-laborers of the printing-office, was a fitting close of such a life,— a glorious sunset.— *Dorchester Beacon.*

Rev. Thomas J. Mumford, editor of *The Christian Register*, who died on Wednesday, was well known to the people of the Unitarian denomination in this vicinity. During Rev. Mr. Moors' absence when a chaplain in the army, Rev. Mr. Mumford had charge of his parish, and endeared himself to all with whom he came in contact. — *Gazette and Courier (Greenfield, Mass.).*

The Christian Register of last week is a memorial number, devoted largely to a review of the life and character of its late editor, Rev. Thomas J. Mumford, whose death was so great a loss to that journal, and to the ministerial and editorial professions. The *Register*, under his management, was one of the brightest and most readable weeklies in the country.— *Golden Rule.*

The death of Thomas J. Mumford, editor of *The Christian Register*, takes from the fraternity one who will be widely and greatly missed. His geniality made the *Register* in spirit thoroughly Christian; lively without being pert, and keen without being sharp-edged. His death was sudden. It will not be easy to find one to fill his place. — *Christian Union.*

We announce with deep sorrow the very sudden death of Rev. Thomas J. Mumford, editor of *The Christian Register*, the Boston Unitarian paper. He was a most genial writer, and for years past we have regarded his paper as the best edited religious weekly of our acquaintance. — *New Covenant.*

He was an earnest anti-slavery worker during that contest, always a friend of humanity and a man of integrity. During his seven years' editorship of the *Register*, he made it a valuable literary paper, and one whose moral influence was of a high order. — *Morning Star.*

Under his auspices, the *Register* has been an exceedingly interesting and readable paper. No one, however widely he might differ from its views, could fail to recognize the vivacity and ability with which they were maintained. — *National Baptist.*

The death of the editor of *The Christian Register* is announced. He was originally an Episcopalian. The *Register*, a Unitarian paper, was considered, under his management, one of the best edited papers in the country. — *Star in the West.*

He always cherished a love for the press, contracted by some editorial experience while yet uncertain as to his vocation. He took charge of the *Register* seven or eight years ago, and has made it an admirable paper. — *Evangelist.*

He was one of the best journalists in the land. — *Methodist.*

"In the room
Of this grief-shadowed Present, there shall be
A Present in whose reign no grief shall gnaw
The heart, and never shall a tender tie
Be broken; in whose reign the eternal Change
That waits on growth and action shall proceed,
With everlasting Concord hand in hand."

BRYANT, The Flood of Years.

www.ingramcontent.com/pod-product-compliance
Lightning Source LLC
Chambersburg PA
CBHW030115030726
47498CB00007B/2395